WHY
WE
TOOK
THE CAR

WHY WE TOOK THE CAR

WOLFGANG HERRNDORF
TRANSLATED BY TIM MOHR

ANDERSEN PRESS • LONDON

Originally published as *Tschick* in 2010 by
Rowohlt.Berlin Verlag GmbH

This edition first published in 2014 by
Andersen Press Limited
20 Vauxhall Bridge Road
London SW1V 2SA

www.andersenpress.co.uk

4 6 8 10 9 7 5 3

British Library Cataloguing in Publication Data available.

ISBN 978 1 78344 031 3

Printed and bound in Great Britain by
CPI Group (UK) Ltd, Croydon CR0 4YY

TO MY FRIENDS

The first thing is the smell of blood and coffee. The coffee machine is sitting over on the table, and the blood is in my shoes. And if I'm being completely honest, I have to admit it's not just blood. When the old guy said "fourteen," I pissed my pants. I'd been sitting there slumped in the chair, not moving. I was dizzy. I tried to look the way I imagined Tschick would look if someone said "fourteen" to him, and then I got so scared I pissed myself. Mike Klingenberg, hero. I have no idea why I'm freaking out now. It was clear the whole time that it would end this way. And you can be sure Tschick wouldn't piss his pants.

Where is Tschick, anyway? I'd last seen him on the side of the autobahn, hopping into the bushes on one leg. But I figure they must have caught him too. You're not going to get far on one leg. Obviously I can't ask the police where he is. Better not bring it up at all in case they hadn't seen him. Maybe they really hadn't seen him. There's no way they're going to find out about him from me. Even if they torture me. Though I don't think German police are allowed to torture people. They only do that on TV. And in Turkey.

But sitting in your own piss and blood in a highway police station and answering questions about your parents isn't exactly the greatest thing ever. In fact, maybe getting tortured would be preferable — at least then I'd have an excuse for freaking out.

The best thing to do is to keep your mouth shut. That's what Tschick said. And that's exactly how I see it too. Especially now, when it doesn't matter anyway. Nothing matters to me at this point. Well, almost nothing. Tatiana Cosic still matters to me, of course. Despite the fact that I haven't thought about her in quite a while now. But as I'm sitting there in the chair and the autobahn is rushing past outside and the older policeman has spent the last five minutes fumbling around with the coffee machine, filling it with water and emptying it out again, flipping the power switch on and off, and looking at the bottom of the machine, when it's obvious to any moron that the extension cord isn't plugged in, I find myself thinking about Tatiana. Even though she had nothing to do with the whole thing. Is what I'm saying here hard to follow? Yeah, well, sorry. I'll try again later. Tatiana isn't even part of the story. The prettiest girl in the world isn't part of the story. Throughout the entire trip, I'd imagined that she could see us. How we'd gazed out from the high point of that field of grain. How we'd stood on top of that mountain of trash with our bundle of plastic hoses, like the last idiots left on Earth . . . I'd always imagined Tatiana was standing behind us, seeing what we saw, smiling when we smiled. But now I'm happy that I only imagined that.

The policeman pulls a green paper towel out of a dispenser and hands it to me. What am I supposed to do with it? Wipe the floor? He grabs his nose with two fingers and looks at me.

Aha. Blow my nose. I blow my nose and he smiles helpfully. I guess I can forget about the whole torture thing. But where should I put the paper towel now? I scan the room. The entire floor of the station is covered with gray linoleum, exactly the same stuff as in the hallways of our school gymnasium. It smells a bit similar too. Piss, sweat, and linoleum. I picture Mr. Wolkow, our gym teacher, sprinting down the hall in his track-suit, with seventy years of workouts behind him: "Let's go, people, hop to it!" The sound of his footsteps smacking the floor, distant giggles from the girls' locker room, Wolkow turning to look in that direction. I picture the tall windows, the bleachers, the rings that never get used dangling from the ceiling. I picture Natalie and Lena and Kimberley coming in through the side entrance of the gym. And Tatiana in her green sweats. I picture their blurry reflections on the floor of the gym, the sparkly pants the girls all wear these days, their tops. And how lately half of them show up for gym in thick wool sweaters and another couple have doctor's notes. Hagecius Junior High School, Berlin, eighth grade.

"I thought it was fifteen," I say, and the policeman shakes his head.

"Nope, fourteen. What's with the coffee machine, Horst?"

"It's broken," says Horst.

I want to talk to my lawyer.

That's the sentence I probably need to say. It's the right sentence in the right situation, as everybody knows from watching TV. And it's easy to say: I want to talk to my lawyer. But they'd probably die laughing. Here's the problem: I have no idea what this sentence means. If I say I want to talk to my lawyer and they ask me, "*Who* do you want to talk to? *Your*

lawyer?" what am I supposed to answer? I've never seen a lawyer in my life, and I don't even know what I need one for. I
don't know if there's a difference between a lawyer and an
attorney. Or an attorney general. I guess they're like judges
except on my side. I guess they know a lot more about the law
than I do. But I guess pretty much everyone in the room knows
more about the law than I do. First and foremost the police-
men. And I could ask them. But I'll bet that if I ask the younger
one if I could use some kind of lawyer right about now, he'll
just turn to his partner and yell, "Hey, Horst! Horsty! Get a
load of this. Our hero here wants to know if he needs a lawyer!
Bleeding all over the floor, pissing himself like a champ, and
wants to talk to *his lawyer*!" Ha, ha, ha. They'd laugh themselves silly. And I figure I'm bad enough off as it is. No reason
to make an even bigger ass of myself. What's done is done.
Nothing else is going to happen now. And a lawyer can't
change that. Whether or not we caused some bad shit is a question only a lunatic would try to argue. What am I supposed to
say? That I spent the entire week lying next to the pool, just
ask the cleaning lady? That all those pig parts must have just
fallen from the sky like rain? There's really not much more I
can do. I could pray in the direction of Mecca, and I could
take a crap in my pants, but otherwise there aren't many
options left.

The younger officer, who actually looks like a nice guy,
shakes his head again and says, "Fifteen? No way. Fourteen.
You're criminally accountable at fourteen."

I should probably have feelings of guilt at this point,
remorse and all that, but to be honest I don't feel a thing. I'm
just unbelievably dizzy. I reach down and scratch my calf,

except that down where my calf used to be, nothing's there. My hand is streaked with violet red slime when I pull it back up. That's not *my* blood, I'd said earlier when they asked. There was enough other slime in the street for them to worry about — and I really didn't think it was my blood. But if it isn't my blood, I ask myself now, where is my calf?

I lift my pant leg and look down. I have exactly one second to think. If I had to watch this in a movie, I think to myself, I would definitely throw up. And sure enough I'm getting sick now, in this oddly calming highway police station. For a split second I see my reflection on the linoleum floor coming toward me, then it smacks into me and I'm out.

The doctor opens and closes his mouth like a carp. It takes a few seconds before words come out. The doctor is yelling. Why is the doctor yelling? He yells at the small woman. Then someone in a uniform steps in, a blue uniform. A policeman, one I don't know yet. The cop shouts at the doctor. How do I even know he's a doctor? He's wearing a white coat. So I guess he could also be a baker. But in the pocket of the coat is a metal flashlight and some kind of listening device. What would a baker need something like that for — to listen for a heartbeat in a bread roll? It's got to be a doctor. And this doctor is pointing at my head now and shouting. I feel around under the sheet where my legs are. They're bare. Don't feel like they're covered in piss or blood anymore. Where am I?

I'm lying on my back. Above me everything is yellow. Glance to the side: big dark window. Other side: white plastic curtain. A hospital, I'd say. The doctor would make sense then too. And, oh yeah, the small woman is also wearing scrubs and carrying a notebook. What hospital — Charité? No, no. I have no idea. I'm not in Berlin. I'll have to ask, I think to myself, but nobody is paying any attention to me. The policeman doesn't like the way the doctor is shouting at him, and he's shouting back. But the doctor just shouts even louder, and interestingly enough you can see who is calling the shots here. The doctor apparently has the authority, not the policeman. I'm worn out and also somehow happy and tired; it feels as if I'm bursting from within with happiness, and I fall back to sleep without saying a single word. The happiness, I find out later, is called Valium. It's administered with big needles.

When I next wake up, it's all bright. The sun is shining in the big window. Something is scratching at the soles of my feet. Aha, a doctor, a different one, and he has another nurse with him. No police. The only unpleasant thing is the doctor scratching at my feet. Why is he doing that?

"He's awake," says the nurse. Not exactly a genius.

"Ah, aha," says the doctor looking at me. "And how do you feel?"

I want to say something, but the only thing that comes out of my mouth is, "Pfff."

"How do you feel? Do you know your name?"

"Pfff-fay?"

What the hell kind of question is that? Do they think I'm crazy or something? I look at the doctor and he looks at me; then he leans over me and shines a flashlight in my eyes. Is this an interrogation? Am I supposed to confess my name? Is this the torture hospital? And if it is, could he just stop lifting up my eyelids for a second and at least pretend he's interested in my answer? Of course, I don't answer anyway. Because, while I'm deciding whether I should say Mike Klingenberg or just Mike or Klinge or Attila the Hun — that's what my father says whenever he's stressed, when he's gotten nothing but bad news all day; he drinks two shots of Jägermeister and answers the phone as Attila the Hun — I mean, as I'm deciding whether to say anything at all or to skip it altogether given the situation, the doctor starts saying something about "four of these" and "three of these" and I pass out again.

There's a lot of things you can say about hospitals, but you can't say they're not nice. I always love being in the hospital. You do nothing all day long, and then the nurses come in. They're all super young and super friendly. And they wear those thin white outfits that I love because you can always see what kind of underwear they have on underneath. Just why I think that's so cool, I'm not sure. Because if they wore those outfits on the street, I'd think it was stupid. But inside a hospital it's great. I think so, anyway. It's a little like those mafia movies, when there's a long silence before one gangster answers another, and they just stare at each other. "Hey!" A minute of silence. "Look me in the eyes!" Five minutes of silence. In regular life that would be stupid. But when you're in the mafia, it's not.

My favorite nurse is from Lebanon and is named Hanna. Hanna has short dark hair and wears normal underwear. And that's cool: *normal underwear.* Other kinds of underwear always look a bit sad. On most people. If you don't have Megan Fox's body, it can look a little desperate. I don't know. Maybe I'm weird, but I like normal underwear.

Hanna is actually still studying to be a nurse. This is her residency or whatever. Before she comes into my room she always pokes her head around the corner and then taps on the door frame with two fingers. Which I think is very thoughtful. And she comes up with a new name for me every day. First I was Mike, then Mikey, then Mikeypikey — which I thought sounded like some old Finnish name. But that wasn't the end. I was Michael Schumacher and Attila the Hun, then pig killer, and finally *the sick bunny*. For that alone I'd love to stay here in the hospital for a year.

Hanna changes my bandages every day. It hurts pretty bad, and I can see from the look on her face that it hurts her to cause me pain too.

"The most important thing is for you to be comfortable," she always says when she's finished. And then I always say I'm going to marry her one day or whatever. Unfortunately she already has a boyfriend. Sometimes she just comes by and sits on the side of my bed because I don't really get any other visitors, and we have great conversations. Real adult conversations. It's so much easier to talk with women like Hanna than with girls my age. If anyone can tell me why that is, I'd love to hear it, because I sure can't figure it out.

The doctor is less talkative. "It's just a piece of flesh," he says. "Muscle," he says. "No big deal, it'll grow back, there'll just be a little indentation or scarring," he says. "It'll look sexy." And he says this every day. Every day he looks at the bandages and tells me the same thing — there'll be a scar, that it's no big deal, that it'll look as if I fought in a war. "As if you've been to war, young man, and women like that," he says, and he says it in a way that's supposed to sound somehow profound. But I don't understand whatever the deep meaning is. Then he winks at me, and I usually wink back even though I don't understand. The man has helped me out, after all, so I can help him out too.

Later on, our conversations improve, mostly because they become more serious. Though actually it's just one conversation. Once I'm able to limp around, he takes me to his office — which, oddly enough, has only a desk and no medical devices — and we sit across the desk from each other like a couple of CEOs closing a deal. On the desk is a plastic model of a human torso with removable organs. The large intestine looks like a brain, and the paint on the stomach is peeling.

"I need to talk to you," says the doctor, which has got to be the stupidest beginning to a conversation that I can possibly imagine. I wait for him to start talking, but unfortunately when someone begins a conversation that way they never start talking right away — somehow *I need to talk to you* and not talking always go together. The doctor stares at me and then drops his gaze and opens a green folder. He doesn't throw it open; he carefully opens it the way I imagine he would peel open the stomach of a patient on the operating table. Cautiously, deftly, very seriously. The man is a surgeon after all. Congratulations on that, by the way, I'm sure someone's real proud.

What comes next is less interesting. Basically he wants to know how I got my head injury. Also where I got my other injuries — from the autobahn, as I had already explained, okay, okay, he knew that already. But the head injury, yeah, well, I fell off my chair at the police station.

The doctor puts the fingers of his hands together. Yes, that's what it says in the report: Fell from chair. At the police station.

He nods. Yes.

I nod too.

"It's just us here," he says after a pause.

"I see that," I say like an idiot, and wink first at the doctor and then for good measure at the plastic torso.

"You don't have to be worried about saying anything here. I'm your doctor, and that means our conversations are completely confidential."

"Okay," I say. He'd said something similar to me a few days before, and now I understand. The man is sworn to secrecy and he wants me to tell him something that he can keep secret. But what? How unbelievably cool it is to piss your pants out of fear?

"It's not just a question of misconduct. It's also a question of negligence. They shouldn't have taken you at your word, do you understand? They should have examined you and called a doctor immediately. Do you know how critical your condition was? And you say you *fell off the chair*?"

"Yes."

"I'm sorry, but doctors are a skeptical bunch. I mean, they wanted something from you. And as your attending doctor . . ."

Yeah, yeah. For God's sake. Confidentiality. I get it. What does he want to know? How someone falls off a chair? Sideways, down, and plop. He shakes his head for a long time; then he makes a small gesture with his hand — and suddenly I understand what he's trying to figure out. My God, I'm so slow sometimes. So damn embarrassing. Why didn't he just ask?

"No, no!" I shout, waving my hands wildly in the air like I'm swatting a swarm of flies. "It was all legit! I was sitting in the chair and I lifted up my pant leg to look at it, and when I did I got all dizzy and fell over. There were no *external factors*." Good phrase. Learned it from a police show.

"Are you sure?"

"I'm sure, yes. The police were actually really nice. They gave me a glass of water and tissues. I just got dizzy and fell over." I straighten myself up in front of the desk and then demonstrate like a talented actor, twice letting myself slump to the right until I nearly fall over.

"Very well," says the doctor slowly.

He scribbles something on a piece of paper.

"I just wanted to know. It was still irresponsible. The blood loss . . . they really should have . . . and it did look suspicious."

He closes the green folder and looks at me for a long time. "I don't know, maybe it's none of my business, but I'd really be interested to know — though you don't have to answer if you don't want to. But what did you want — or where were you trying to go?"

"I have no idea."

"Like I said, you don't have to answer. I'm only asking out of curiosity."

"I would tell you, but if I did, you wouldn't believe me anyway. I'm pretty sure."

"I'd believe you," he says with a friendly smile. My buddy.

"It's stupid."

"What's stupid?"

"It's just . . . well, we were trying to go to Wallachia. See, I told you you'd think it was stupid."

"I don't think it's stupid, I just don't understand. *Where* were you trying to go?"

"Wallachia."

"And where is that supposed to be?"

He looks at me curiously, and I can tell I'm turning red. We're not going to delve any deeper into this. We shake each other's hands like grown men, signaling an end to the conversation, and I'm somehow happy that I didn't have to push the bounds of his confidentiality.

I've never had any nicknames. In school, I mean. Or anywhere else, for that matter. My name is Mike Klingenberg. Mike. Not Mikey or Klinge or anything like that. Always just Mike. Except in the sixth grade, when I was briefly known as Psycho. Not like that's the greatest thing either, being called Psycho. But it didn't last long and then I was back to being Mike again.

When someone doesn't have any nicknames, it's for one of two reasons. Either you're incredibly boring and don't get any because of that, or you don't have any friends. If I had to decide between one or the other, I'd have to say I'd rather have no friends than be incredibly boring. I mean, if you're boring you won't have any friends anyway, or you'll only have friends who are even more boring than you are.

But there is one other possibility: You could be boring *and* have no friends. And I'm afraid that's my problem. At least since Paul moved away. Paul had been my friend since kinder-garten, and we used to hang out almost every day — until his dumbass mother decided she wanted to live out in the country.

That was about the time I started junior high, and it didn't make things any easier. I hardly saw Paul at all after that. His new place was half a world away, at the last stop of one of the subway lines and then six more kilometers by bike from there. And Paul changed out there. His parents split up and he went nuts. I mean really crazy. Paul basically lives in the forest with his mother and just lies around brooding. He always had a tendency to do that anyway. You really had to push him to do anything. But out there in the middle of nowhere, there's nobody to push him, so he just stews. If I remember right, I visited him three times out there. He was so depressed every time that I never wanted to go again. Paul showed me the house, the yard, the woods, and a hunting blind in the woods where he'd sit and watch animals. Except, of course, that there were no animals. Every few hours a sparrow flew by. And he jotted down notes about that. It was early in the year, right when *Grand Theft Auto IV* came out, though Paul wasn't interested in that kind of thing anymore. Nothing interested him except wild critters. I had to spend an entire day up in a tree, and then the whole thing just became too idiotic for me. Once I also secretly flipped through his notebook to see what else was in it — because there was a lot in it. Things about his mother, things written in some kind of secret code, drawings of naked women — terrible drawings. Nothing against naked women. Naked women are awesome. But these drawings were not awesome. They were just messed up. And between the sketches, in calligraphy, observations about animals and the weather. At some point he'd written that he'd seen wild boars and lynxes and wolves. There was a question mark next to the word *wolves*, and I said to him, "This is the outskirts of Berlin — lynxes and wolves, are you sure?" And he grabbed the book out of my hand and looked at me as if *I* was the crazy one. After that we didn't see each other very often. That was three years ago. And he'd once been my best friend.

I didn't get to know anybody in junior high at first. I'm not exactly great at getting to know people. And I never saw it as a major problem. Until Tatiana Cosic showed up. Or at least until I noticed her. She'd been in my class the whole time. I just never noticed her until the seventh grade. No idea why. But in seventh grade she suddenly popped up on my radar — and that's when all my misery began. I guess at this point I should probably describe Tatiana. Because otherwise the rest of the story won't make sense.

Tatiana's first name is Tatiana and her last name is Cosic. She's fourteen years old and her parents' last name is also Cosic. I don't know what their first names are. They're from Serbia or Croatia, you can tell from their last name, and they live in a white apartment building with lots of windows. Yadda, yadda, yadda.

I could blather on about her for ages, but the surprising thing is that I actually have no idea what I'm talking about. I don't know Tatiana at all. I know the things that anyone in her class would know about her. I know what she looks like, what her name is, and that she's good at sports and English. And so on. I know how tall she is because of the physical exams they gave us on health day. I found out where she lives from the phone book. And other than that, I know basically nothing. Obviously I could describe exactly what she looks like and how her voice sounds and what color her hair is and everything. But that seems to me unnecessary. I mean, everyone can imagine what she looks like: she looks great. Her voice sounds great too. She's just great all around.

17

I guess I never explained why they called me Psycho. Because,
as I mentioned, I was known as Psycho for a while. No idea
what the point was. I mean, obviously I know it was supposed
to suggest that I had a screw loose. But as far as I'm concerned,
there were several other people who deserved the name more
than I did. Frank could have been called Psycho, or Stobke,
with his lighter. They're both way crazier than I am. Or the
Nazi. But then again, the Nazi was already called Nazi, so he
didn't need another name. And of course there was a reason
that I got the name instead of anyone else. It was the result of
an assignment in Mr. Schuermann's German class, sixth grade,
a word prompt story. In case you don't know what a word
prompt story is, it goes like this: You get four words, like
"zoo," "ape," "zookeeper," and "hat," and you have to write a
story that includes all of the words. Real original. Totally
moronic. The words Mr. Schuermann thought up were "vacation," "water," "rescue," and "God." Which was definitely
more difficult than zoo and ape. The main difficulty was God,
obviously. We only had ethics classes, not religion, and there
were sixteen kids registered as atheists in the class, including
me. Even the Protestants in the class didn't really believe in

God. I don't think. At least, not the way people who *really* believe in God believe. People who don't want to harm even an ant, or who are happy when someone dies because that person is going to heaven. Or people who crash a plane into the World Trade Center. Those people really believe in God. That's why the writing assignment was tough. Most of the students grabbed on to the word "vacation." A little family is paddling around off the Côte d'Azur and are taken totally by surprise by a terrible storm and yell "oh, God" and are then rescued or whatever. And I could have written something like that too. But as I sat down to write the story, the first thing that occurred to me was the fact that we hadn't been on vacation for three years because my father had been preparing for bankruptcy. Which didn't bother me — I never particularly liked going on vacation with my parents anyway.

Instead, I spent last summer squatting in our basement carving boomerangs. One of my elementary school teachers taught me how to do it. He was an expert in the boomerang department. Bretfeld was his name, Wilhelm Bretfeld. He'd even written a book about boomerangs. Two books actually. But I didn't realize that until after I'd finished elementary school. I ran into old Bretfeld in a field. He was basically standing right behind our house in the cow pasture throwing his boomerangs, homemade boomerangs he'd carved himself. It was yet another thing I had never realized really worked. I thought the things only came back to you in the movies. But Bretfeld was a pro, and he showed me how to do it. I was blown away. Also because he'd made them himself. "Anything that's round in front and sharp at the back will fly," said Bretfeld. Then he looked at me over the frames of his glasses and asked,

"What's your name again? I can't remember you." The thing that most blew my mind was the long-distance boomerang. He'd developed it himself. It could fly for ages — and he had *invented* it. All over the world today, when someone throws a boomerang and it stays in the air for five minutes, setting some record, and a picture is taken of it, it's always there: *based on a design by Wilhelm Bretfeld*. He's world renowned, Bretfeld. And he was standing in the field behind our house last summer and showed me how to do it. A really good teacher. Though I never noticed it in elementary school.

In any event, I spent the entire summer break sitting in the basement whittling. And it was a great summer break, much better than going somewhere on vacation. My parents were almost never home. My father drove around from creditor to creditor and my mother was at the beauty farm. And that's what I wrote the assignment about: *Mother and the Beauty Farm*, a word prompt story by Mike Klingenberg.

The next class, I got to read it aloud. Or I had to. I didn't want to. Svenja was first up, and she had written one of those nonsense stories about the Côte d'Azur, which Schuermann thought was great. Then Kevin read basically the same story except that instead of the Côte d'Azur it was the Baltic coast. Then it was my turn. Mother at the beauty farm. It's not really a beauty farm. Though my mother does always look better when she comes back from it. It's actually a clinic. She's an alcoholic. She's drunk booze for as long as I can remember, but the difference is that it used to be funnier. Everyone is normally funny when they drink, but when a certain line is crossed people get tired or aggressive. And when my mother started walking around our place with a kitchen knife again, I was standing upstairs with my father as he called down, "How about another trip to the beauty farm?" That's how the summer started at the end of sixth grade.

I like my mother. I have to add that, because what I'm about to say might not cast her in the best light. But I always liked her, and still do. She's not like other moms. That's what I've always liked best about her. She can be really funny, for instance, and you can't say that about most mothers. Calling the clinic the beauty farm was one of her jokes.

My mother used to play a lot of tennis. My father too, but not very well. The ace in our family was my mother. When she was still in shape, she won the tennis club championship every year. She even won it with a bottle of vodka in her system, but that's another story. Anyway, as a kid I was always at the courts with her. My mother sat on the terrace at the tennis club and drank cocktails with Frau Weber and Frau Osterthun and Herr Schuback and the rest of them. And I sat under the table and played with Matchbox cars as the sun shone down. In my mind the sun was always shining at the tennis club. I looked at the red clay dust on five sets of white tennis shoes and collected bottle caps — you could draw on the insides of the caps with a ballpoint pen. I was allowed to have five ice creams a day and ten cans of Coke and could just tell the waiter to add it to our tab. And then Frau Weber said, "Next week at seven again, Frau Klingenberg?"

And my mother: "Sure."

And Frau Weber: "I'll bring the balls next time."

My mother: "Sure."

And so on and so forth. Always the same conversation. Though the joke was that Frau Weber never brought balls — she was too cheap.

Once in a while there was another version. It went like this:

"Again next Saturday, Frau Klingenberg?"

"Can't do it. I'll be away."

"But doesn't your husband's team have a league match?"

"Yes, but he's not going to be away. I am."

"Aha. Where are you going?"

"To the beauty farm."

And then somebody at the table who didn't know the phrase yet always, always, always, threw out the unbelievably clever quip, "You certainly don't need any help in that department, Frau Klingenberg."

Then my mother would knock back the rest of her Brandy Alexander and say, "That was only a joke, Herr Schuback. It's actually a rehab facility."

Then we would walk home hand in hand because my mother was no longer capable of driving. I carried her heavy racquet bag and she said to me, "You can't learn much from your mother. But two things you can learn: First, you can talk about anything. Second, what people think doesn't mean shit." That was enlightening. Talk openly. Screw what other people think.

My doubts crept in only later. Not doubts about the ideas in principle. But doubts about whether my mother really didn't care what other people thought.

Anyway, the beauty farm. I don't know exactly what went on there. Because I was never allowed to visit my mother. She didn't want me to. But whenever she came home from the place she told the craziest stories. The therapy apparently consisted of talking a lot and not drinking. And sometimes exercise as well. But most of them couldn't really do much exercise. For the most part they talked while tossing a ball of yarn around in a circle. The person allowed to speak was the person with the ball of yarn. I had to ask about the ball of yarn five times because I wasn't sure whether I'd heard it right or whether maybe it was a joke. But it was no joke. My mother didn't think this detail was so funny or fascinating, but to be honest I found it incredibly fascinating. Just try to imagine it: ten adults sitting in a circle and throwing a ball of yarn around. Afterward, the entire room was full of yarn, but that wasn't the point of the whole thing, even if it's fair to think so at first. The point was to create a *web of communication*. Which tells you that my mother wasn't the craziest person in the place. There must have been considerably crazier ones too.

But anyone who thinks the ball of yarn must be the strangest thing at the clinic hasn't heard about the cardboard boxes. Every patient had a cardboard box. It hung from the ceiling in each room, with the open side facing up. You had to throw notes into the box, basketball style. Notes where you wrote your aspirations, wishes, resolutions, prayers, or whatever. Whenever my mother wished for something, made a resolution, or scolded herself, she wrote it down on a piece of paper, folded it up, and then basically did a Dirk Nowitzki and slam-dunked it in the cardboard box. And the insane thing about it was that nobody ever read them. That wasn't the point. The point was just writing it down so it was there and you could see it — *my desires and wishes and all that crap are hanging right there in that box*. And because the cardboard boxes were so important, you had to give them names. The name was written on the box with a felt-tip marker, so basically every drunkard had a box named "God" hanging from the ceiling with all his or her aspirations inside it. Because most people just called their box God. That's what the therapists suggested — just call it God. But you were allowed to call it whatever you wanted. Some old lady called hers "Osiris" and somebody else "Great Spirit."

My mother named her box "Karl-Heinz," and as a result a therapist came and peppered her with questions. The first thing he wanted to know was whether it was her father. "Who?" she asked, and the therapist pointed at the box hanging from the ceiling. My mother shook her head. Then the therapist asked just who he was, this Karl-Heinz. And my mother said, "That cardboard box." So then the therapist asked what the name of her father was. "Gottlieb," she said, to which the therapist said, "Aha!" It was supposed to sound clever, as if the therapist had just figured something out. Gottlieb, aha! My mother had no idea what the therapist had figured out, and he never said. And that's the way it went the entire time. They all tried like crazy to act as if they had things figured out, but they never gave away what they knew. When my father heard about it — the thing with the cardboard box — he nearly fell out of his chair laughing. He kept saying, "My God that's sad," though he was laughing. So I had to laugh too, and my mother decided it was funny as well, at least in retrospect.

And I put all of that into my school essay. And in order to get the word "rescue" in, I added the scene with the kitchen knife. And since I was on a roll, I even added a bit about how she mistook me for my father when she came down the stairs one morning. It was the longest assignment I'd ever written — at least eight pages long — and still I could have written a Part Two, a Part Three, and a Part Four if I'd felt like it. Though as I found out, Part One was more than enough.

The class totally lost it while I was reading it aloud. Schuermann told everyone to quiet down and then said, "Nice, very nice. How much longer is it? Still so much to go? That'll do for now, I'd say." I didn't have to read the rest. Schuermann had me stay after class so he could read the rest of it on his own, and I stood there next to him feeling very proud — first because it had been such a success and second because Schuermann wanted to read the whole thing personally. Mike Klingenberg, author. And then Schuermann closed the notebook I'd written my assignment in and shook his head. I took it as an appreciative shake of the head, the kind that signals, *How can a sixth grader write such an incredibly great essay?* But then he said, "Why are you grinning like an idiot? Do you think this is funny?" And it slowly dawned on me that it hadn't been such a success after all. At least not as far as Schuermann was concerned.

He got up from his desk, walked over to the window, and stood there looking out at the schoolyard. "Mike," he said, turning around again to face me. "That's your *mother*. Did you ever stop to think about that?"

Obviously I'd made a huge mistake. I just didn't know what it was. But it was clear from Schuermann's reaction that I'd committed an absolutely massive error with my assignment. And that he thought it was the most embarrassing essay the world had ever witnessed. But I couldn't figure out why this was the case — he never said, and to be honest I don't know why to this day. He just kept repeating that it was my *mother*, until he suddenly started getting very loud and said my assignment was the most sickening, unsavory, and shameless one he'd encountered in fifteen years of teaching — blah, blah, blah — and that I should immediately rip the pages out of my notebook. I was totally devastated, and of course I reached straight for my notebook, like a moron, to rip out the pages. But Schuermann grabbed my hand and shouted, "I don't mean literally rip it out. Don't you understand anything? What you need to do is think hard about what you've done. Really think!" I thought for a minute about it, but to be honest I just didn't get it. I still don't get it. I mean, it's not as if I made any of it up or anything.

CHAPTER SEVEN

After that I was called Psycho. For almost a year, everyone called me that. Even in class. Even when the teacher was there. "Come on, Psycho, pass the ball! You can do it, Psycho! Chill out, Psycho!" And it only stopped when André landed in our class. André Langin. Handsome André.

André had been held back. He had a girlfriend by the end of his first day in our class. And he had a new one every week after that. These days he's with a Turkish girl who looks like Salma Hayek. He was sniffing around Tatiana for a little while too, and it drove me nuts. For a few days they were talking to each other constantly — in the hall, in front of school, in the schoolyard. But in the end they didn't get together, I don't think. That would have killed me. At some point they stopped talking to each other, and shortly afterward I heard André explain to Patrick why men and women don't get along — crazy scientific theories about the Stone Age, saber-toothed tigers, and childbirth and all that. I hated him for that too. I hated him from the very first moment, though it wasn't easy for me. For one thing, even though André's not the brightest bulb, he's not a complete waste of space. He can be nice too, and he's pretty laid-back. And, like I mentioned, he's decent

27

looking. But he's still an asshole. And just to make it worse, he lives only a block away from me, at 15 Wald Street. The house is full of assholes, by the way. The Langins have a giant place. His father's a politician, city councilman or something. Of course. And my father says, "Langin thinks he's Mr. Big Man!"

But to get back to the story I meant to tell, when André was brand-new in our class, we took a field trip to go hiking somewhere south of Berlin. Just a standard nature walk in the woods. I trailed way behind the others and actually tried to take in the nature. This was around the time we had planted an herb garden, and I was genuinely interested in nature for a while there. Interested in *trees*. I was thinking of becoming a scientist or something. But not for long, and it probably had something to do with that field trip, where I hung back so I could examine the leaf patterns and growth forms in peace. That's when it suddenly occurred to me that I didn't give the slightest crap about leaf patterns and growth forms. Ahead of me everyone was laughing and having fun, and I could make out Tatiana Cosic's laugh from the rest; two hundred meters behind, Mike Klingenberg was traipsing through the forest looking at fucking leaf patterns in nature. Which wasn't even really nature. It was just some crappy woods with educational plaques posted every ten meters. Hell.

At some stage we stopped at a three-hundred-year-old white beech tree that had been planted there by Frederick the Great. The teacher asked who knew what kind of tree it was. Nobody knew. Except me, of course. But I wasn't so crazy as to admit in front of the whole class that I knew it was a white beech. I might as well have said, "My name is Psycho and I have a problem." It was depressing that we were all standing

28

around the tree and not a single person knew what it was. I'm getting to the point now. Beneath this white beech tree Frederick the Great had also put a few tables and benches so people could sit and picnic. Which is exactly what we did. By coincidence I ended up at a table with Tatiana Cosic. Opposite me was André, handsome André, with his arms stretched out right and left around the shoulders of Laura and Marie. As if he were best friends with them. Except that he wasn't friends with them at all. He'd been in our class for maybe a week at that stage. But the two of them didn't object. On the contrary, they seemed to be frozen with excitement and didn't move a muscle. It was as if they were afraid his arms would, like skittish birds, get spooked if they moved their shoulders. André didn't say anything at all. He just looked around with his bedroom eyes. And then he glanced at me and, after thinking for a while, said to nobody in particular but definitely not to me, "Why is this guy called Psycho anyway? He's totally boring." Laura and Marie laughed themselves silly over this top-quality joke, and since it had been such a success, André repeated it: "Seriously, why is this walking sleeping pill named Psycho?" And ever since then, I've been Mike again. And it's even worse than before.

There are a lot of things I'm no good at. But if there's one thing I can do, it's the high jump. I mean, okay, I'm not an Olympic athlete, but I'm still pretty close to unbeatable at high jump and long jump. Even though I'm one of the shortest kids, I get as high as Olaf, the tallest kid in our class. Early in the year I set a record for our age group, and I was really proud. We were standing at the high jump bar, and the girls were all sitting around on the grass nearby, where Frau Bielcke was giving them a lecture. Frau Bielcke blathers on and the girls just sit there scratching their ankles. They don't constantly run around the track like we have to with Mr. Wolkow.

Wolkow is our gym teacher, and he loves to give us lectures too. Every gym teacher I've ever had has let the words fly. With Wolkow, Mondays are reserved for the soccer results, pretty much the same on Tuesdays, Wednesdays he talks about the Champions League, and by Friday he's already looking forward to that weekend's soccer matches and all the analysis surrounding them. In summer he airs his opinions on the Tour de France, but once he starts talking about doping he quickly comes back around to the much more important topic of soccer and the happy fact that there's no doping in that sport.

Because it's of *no use* in soccer. That is Wolkow's honest opinion. But nobody cares anyway because of one basic problem: Wolkow talks only while we're running. He's in insane shape. He must be seventy, and yet he's always out in front of us, loping comfortably and gabbing on and on. And then he always says, "Men!" Then he's silent for about ten meters. Then, "Dortmund." Another ten meters. "Haven't got a chance." Ten more meters. "Home field advantage. Am I right or am I right?" Twenty meters. "And that old fox who coaches Bayern Munich. It's not going to be a walk in the park." Giddyup, giddyup. "What do you all think?" Thirty seconds of silence. Obviously nobody says anything because we've already run like a million loops around the track. Once in a while Hans, the Nazi, who's a knuckle-dragging soccer fan and who is always lagging behind the rest of us, sweating his ass off, yells, "Hey, ho, let's go, Hertha Berlin!" And that's too much even for Wolkow, the old windbag, and he slows down so Hans can catch up, then lifts his pointer finger and yells in a voice quivering with rage, "Joe Simunic! The cardinal sin!" And Hans yells back, "I know, I know." Then Wolkow speeds up again and mumbles to himself, "Simunic, my God! The foundation of the franchise! Never trade the franchise player! And now they've tanked."

Just the fact that we're not forced to listen to him blather is reason enough to get excited about the high jump. Maybe we did the high jump only on days when Wolkow had such a heavy chest cold that he couldn't run and talk at the same time. When he's fighting a normal cold, he still manages to babble, just a bit less than usual. When he's dead, class is canceled. But when he's really sick, he runs silently around the track.

During the high jump he jotted down our results in his black notebook and croaked about how we had managed to clear a few centimeters more the previous year. The girls, like I said, were sitting next to the high jump setup listening to Frau Bielcke. In reality, none of them were listening, of course, and were actually looking over at us.

Tatiana was with her best friend, Natalie, at the outer edge of the group of girls. They crouched down and whispered to each other. It was as if I were sitting on hot coals. I desperately wanted to jump before Frau Bielcke finished her sermon. Luckily Wolkow suddenly made it a contest: The bar was put at one meter and twenty centimeters and anyone who couldn't clear it was out. Then it would be raised in five centimeter increments for each new round. At one meter twenty only Heckel failed. Heckel has a fat gut, has had it since he was in fifth grade. And he has toothpicks for legs. It's no great surprise that he can't get far off the ground. He's not very good in any school subject, but he's particularly crap at sports. He's dyslexic too, which means his spelling doesn't count against him in German class. He can make as many mistakes as he wants. All that counts is the content and the style because dyslexia's like a disease and he can't do anything about it. But I keep thinking that the same is true for his matchstick legs — there's nothing he can do about them. His father is a bus driver and looks exactly the same: a tub on stilts. So really Heckel is high-jump dyslexic too, and how high he gets shouldn't be counted, only his style. But it's not a recognized disease, so he fails gym and all the girls giggle when the tub of lard shields himself from the bar with both hands and falls with a whimper on his face. Poor bastard. Though I have to admit it does look funny. Because even if height were discounted for Heckel, his style is still an F.

By the time we reached one meter forty centimeters, the field began to dwindle. At one meter fifty, the only ones left were Kevin and Patrick, and, with great effort, André. And me, of course. Olaf was sick. When André squeaked over the bar, the girls cheered and celebrated, and Frau Bielcke looked at them sternly. At one meter fifty-five, Natalie shouted, "You can do it, André!" Such a stupid way to cheer him on, since there was no way he could do it. On the contrary, he actually went *under* the bar, which often happens in the high jump when you bite off more than you can chew. He crawled off the back of the cushion and tried to compensate by making a joke as if he was going to throw the bar like a spear. But it's an old joke. Nobody laughed. Next they cheered on Kevin. Kevin the math genius. But he couldn't clear one meter sixty. Then I was the only one left. Wolkow set the bar at one meter sixty-five, and even as I approached it I could just feel that today was my day. It was Mike Klingenberg Day. I could feel a rush of triumph even as I leapt. I didn't jump so much as sail over the bar like an airplane. I hung in the air, I floated. Mike Klingenberg, star of track and field. I think that if I could have given myself a nickname just then, it would have been something like Aeroflot. Or Air Klingenberg. Or the Condor. But unfortunately you can't give yourself nicknames. As my back sank into the soft landing pad, I could hear restrained applause from the side where all the boys were gathered. But from the side where the girls were I heard nothing. As the mat rebounded and I bounced back up, I immediately looked over at Tatiana. And Tatiana was looking at Frau Bielcke. Natalie was looking at

Frau Bielcke too. They hadn't even seen my jump, the stupid cows. None of the girls had seen my jump. They had no interest in what the psychotic sleeping pill had managed to clear. Aeroflot my ass.

It really pissed me off the entire day. Though to be fair it hadn't interested me either. As if the fucking high jump would interest me for even a second! But if André had managed to clear one meter sixty-five — or even if he had managed to get to the point where he could have *attempted* one sixty-five — the girls would have run around the track with pom-poms. For me, on the other hand, not a single one even watched. I'm of no interest. And I just can't help wondering: Why doesn't anyone watch when Air Klingenberg flies over the bar to set a new school record, while everyone watches when some airhead submarines his way under the bar? But that's the way it was. That was what the whole crappy school was like, that was what the girls were like, and there was no way around it. At least that's what I always thought before I met Tschick. That's when things started to change.

Right from the start, Tschick rubbed me the wrong way. I couldn't stand him. Nobody could stand him. Tschick was trash, and that's exactly what he looked like. Mr. Wagenbach dragged him into class after Easter break, and when I say he dragged him into class, I really mean it. It was the first period after the break — history. The students were sitting in their chairs as if stapled in place, because if anyone is an authoritarian asshole, it's Wagenbach. Although asshole is a bit of an overstatement. Wagenbach's okay, actually. He lectures okay and he's not as stupid as most of the rest of them — like Wolkow. At least with Wagenbach it doesn't take a lot of effort to pay attention to what he's saying. And it's a good thing to pay attention, too, because Wagenbach can really rip you to shreds. Everybody knows it. Even kids who've never had him for a class. Before fifth graders even enter Hagecius Junior High they know: Watch out for Wagenbach! You can hear a pin drop in his class. In Schuermann's class, you hear cell phones ring about five times a day. Patrick even managed to change his ringtone during Schuermann's class — he tried out six, seven, eight different ringtones one after the next until finally Schuermann asked for *a little quiet*. And even then he didn't have the nerve to glare at Patrick. If somebody's phone were to ring in Wagenbach's class, whoever it belonged to would definitely not live to see recess. There's even a rumor that Wagenbach used to keep a hammer on his desk to smash cell phones that went off in his class. But I don't know if that's true.

Anyway, as usual, Wagenbach came in wearing a bad suit and carrying his shit-brown briefcase, and behind him he was dragging this kid who looked half-comatose. Wagenbach slammed his briefcase down on his desk and turned around. He waited with a scowl on his face until the boy was standing next to him and said, "We have a new classmate. His name is Andrej . . ."

Then he looked down at a notepad, and at the kid again. Apparently, he wanted the new student to pronounce his own name. But the boy just stood there with his eyes half-closed and stared into the distance without saying anything.

Perhaps it's not worth mentioning what I thought the moment I saw Tschick for the first time, but I want to anyway. I had an extremely bad feeling about him the second I saw him next to Wagenbach. He seemed like just another asshole. Even though I didn't know him at all and had no idea whether he really was an asshole. He was Russian, it turned out. He was average height, had on a dirty white shirt that was missing a button, bargain basement jeans, and misshapen brown shoes that looked like dead rats. He also had extremely high cheek-bones and slits instead of eyes. His eyes — these narrow slits — were the first thing you noticed about him. They made him look Mongolian and you could never tell where he was looking. He had his mouth open a little on one side — like he was smoking an invisible cigarette. His forearms were huge and there was a big scar on one of them. His legs were skinny, and the top of his head was kind of squared off.

Nobody giggled. Nobody ever giggled in Wagenbach's class. But I had the impression that even if we'd been in somebody else's class nobody would have giggled. The Russian just stood there and looked who-knows-where out of his Mongolian eyes. And he completely ignored Wagenbach. It was quite an accomplishment to ignore Wagenbach. It was practically impossible.

"Andrej," Wagenbach said, staring again at the notepad and silently moving his lips. "Andrej Tsch . . . Tschicha . . . tschoroff."

The Russian mumbled something.

"Excuse me?"

"Tschichatschow," said the Russian without looking at Wagenbach.

Wagenbach inhaled through his nostrils. That was one of his quirks. Inhaling through his nostrils.

"Great, Tschischaroff. Andrej. Could you tell us a little bit about yourself? Where you're from, which school you attended previously?"

This was standard. Whenever new students arrived in school, they had to say where they were from or whatever. And now for the first time since he entered the room, Tschick's expression changed. He turned his head slightly toward Wagenbach as if noticing him for the first time. He scratched his neck, turned back toward the class, and said, "No." The room was deathly quiet.

Wagenbach nodded seriously and said, "You don't wish to say where you're from?"

"No," said Tschick. "Who cares?"

"Fine. In that case I will tell the class a bit about you, Andrej. Out of politeness, I would like to introduce you to the class."

He looked at Tschick. Tschick looked at the class.

"I take your silence as consent," said Wagenbach. He said it with an ironic tone the way all teachers do when they say something like that.

Tschick didn't answer.

"Or do you have something against it?" asked Wagenbach.

"Go right ahead," said Tschick with a wave of the hand.

Somewhere a couple of girls started to giggle. *Go right ahead!* Insane. He pronounced each syllable distinctly, with a strange accent. And he was still just staring at the back wall of the classroom. His eyes might even have been closed. It was tough to tell. Wagenbach gave the class a look. And it was absolutely silent again.

"Right," he said. "Andrej Tschicha . . . schoff is the name of our new classmate, and as you can no doubt discern from his name, our guest has come from far away. The boundless Russian expanses, which Napoleon conquered in 1812 and, as we'll see, was soon expelled from again. Just as Charles XII had been before him and Hitler would be after him."

Wagenbach inhaled through his nostrils. The introduction had no impact on Tschick. He didn't move.

"In any event, Andrej came to Germany four years ago with his brother, and . . . Wouldn't you rather explain this yourself?"

The Russian made some sort of sound.

"Andrej, I'm talking to you," said Wagenbach.

"No," said Tschick. "And by no I mean, No, I would not rather tell it myself."

Suppressed laughter. Wagenbach nodded awkwardly.

"Fine, then I will do it, if you have no objection. But this is most unorthodox."

Tschick shook his head.

"It's not unorthodox?"

"No."

"Well, *I* find it unorthodox," insisted Wagenbach. "I think it's admirable to introduce oneself. But in the interest of time, we'll keep this short. Our friend Andrej is from a family of German origin, but his native language is Russian. He's a great communicator, as we can see, but he first learned German when he arrived here in Germany, and as result should be granted understanding in certain . . . in certain areas. Four years ago he started in a special education program. Then he transferred because his grades permitted him to enter a standard school. But he didn't stay there long either — next up was a year at a vocational school and now he's joining us. And all of this in just four years. Is that right so far?"

Tschick rubbed the back of his hand across his nose, then looked at his hand. "Ninety percent," he said.

Wagenbach paused to see if Tschick was going to say anything more. But he didn't. The ten percent discrepancy remained unexplained.

"Alright," said Wagenbach in a surprisingly friendly tone. "No doubt we're all interested to hear the rest of the story, but unfortunately you can't stand up here forever, as enjoyable as it is talking with you. I would like to suggest that you sit at the free desk in the back there, since it's the only one available. Yes?"

Tschick lumbered down the aisle like a robot. Everyone stared at him. Tatiana and Natalie put their heads together, whispering.

"Napoleon!" said Wagenbach. Then he paused dramatically to pull a pack of tissues out of his briefcase and blow his nose at length.

Tschick arrived in the back of class in the meantime, and down the aisle where he had walked wafted a scent that almost knocked me over. A vapor trail of alcohol. I was three seats from the aisle and I could have put together a list of the drinks he'd had in the last twenty-four hours. That was how my mother smelled when she had a bad day. Maybe that was the reason Tschick hadn't faced Wagenbach or opened his mouth — he was worried about the booze on his breath. But Wagenbach had a cold. He couldn't smell anything anyway.

Tschick sat at the free desk in the back row. Kallenbach, the class clown, had started the year there, but he'd been moved to the front row before the end of the first day of school so the teachers could keep him under control. And now, instead, this Russian was sitting in the back row, and I'm sure I wasn't the only one thinking that it hadn't been such a great idea to move Kallenbach now that the Russian was going to end up back there. He was on a totally different level from Kallenbach — that was obvious. And that's why everyone kept turning around to look at him. After his performance with Wagenbach you just knew something was going to happen. This was going to be interesting.

But then nothing happened the rest of the day. Each new teacher who came in greeted Tschick and he had to spell his name at the beginning of every period. But everything went smoothly. The next day was quiet too. It was a major disappointment. He always wore the same ratty shirt to school, didn't participate in class, said "Yes," "No," or "Don't know" whenever he was asked anything, and didn't disturb things. He didn't become friends with anyone. He didn't even try to make friends with anyone. He didn't reek of alcohol the second day, but you still got the impression when you looked at him in the back row that he was somehow out of it. The way he slumped in his chair with his eyes barely open, you never knew whether he was asleep, wasted, or just really laid-back.

But about once a week he would smell like booze again. Not as bad as on that first day, but still obvious. There were some kids in class — myself not included — who had already gotten drunk or high, but for somebody to show up to school in the morning drunk? That was new. Tschick chewed really strong-smelling mint gum whenever he was drunk, so everyone figured out how to tell what state he was in.

But otherwise nobody knew much about him. It was absurd enough that someone would transfer from a special ed program to a school like ours. And then there were his clothes. But there were people who defended him, saying he actually wasn't stupid at all. "At least not as stupid as Kallenbach," I said one time — I was one of the people who defended him. But the only reason I defended him, to be honest, was because Kallenbach was standing next to me and he always got on my nerves. From the things Tschick said, you really couldn't tell whether he was smart or stupid or somewhere in between.

41

Of course there were also rumors about him and his background. Chechnya, Siberia, and Moscow all came up. Kevin said Tschick and his brother lived in a camping trailer on the outskirts of the city, and that his brother was a weapons dealer. Somebody else said he knew for a fact the brother was a pimp and there was talk of a forty-room mansion where the Russian mafia had orgies. Another kid said Tschick lived in one of the old high-rise apartment buildings out toward the big lake, Mueggelsee. The truth was that all of it was a load of crap. And the only reason he generated so many rumors was because Tschick himself never talked to anyone. But for the same reason, he was slowly forgotten. Or at least forgotten as much as someone who comes to school in the same awful shirt and cheap jeans everyday and sits in the class clown's seat can be forgotten. At least the dead animal shoes were replaced by a pair of white Adidas, which, of course, somebody *knew* had just been stolen. And maybe he had stolen them. But the number of rumors surrounding him kept dwindling. The last thing was a nickname for him, which was Tschick. And for those who thought that was too simple, there was also "special ed." And with that, the topic of the Russian was pretty much exhausted. Inside our classroom, at least.

Out in the parking lot he remained a topic of conversation a bit longer. In the morning, kids from the adjacent high school hung out in the parking lot. Some of them already had cars. And they found the Mongolian incredibly interesting. Guys who'd been held back five times and liked to stand in the open doors of their cars, just so everybody could see they were the owners — owners of cars that were hunks of junk, but which were tuned and modified. They made fun of Tschick. "Wasted again, Ivan?" Every morning. Especially one guy with a yellow Ford Fiesta. I didn't know for a long time whether Tschick realized they were making fun of him, but one day he stopped in his tracks at the edge of the parking lot. I was locking up my bike and heard them all loudly taking bets on whether Tschick would manage to make it through the door to the school the way he was staggering. Or as they put it, the way the fucking Mongolian was staggering. And Tschick stopped and went back toward the parking lot and up to the guys doing the talking. They were all a head taller than he was and several years older, and they grinned as the Russian walked up to them — and then past most of them. He went straight up to the Ford Fiesta guy, who was the loudest of all, put his hand on the car door and said something to him so quietly that nobody was able to hear what it was. The grin on the Ford guy's face slowly disappeared and Tschick turned around and went into our school building. After that, nobody made any comments when he walked past.

I wasn't the only one who saw this happen, and from that point on there was no stopping the rumors about his family being in the Russian mafia. Nobody could imagine any other way he could have managed to silence the idiot with the Ford with a couple of sentences. But of course that was baloney. Mafia. Bunch of baloney. That's what I thought, anyway.

Two weeks later we got our first math assignments back. First, Mr. Strahl put the results on the board to scare us. This time there was one A, which was unusual. Strahl's favorite sentence was: "As are reserved for God." Horrifying. But Strahl was a math teacher, after all, meaning he was a madman. There were two Bs, loads of Cs and Ds, no Es. And one F. I had a slight hope that I'd earned the A — math was the only subject I ever managed to score an A in once in a while. But it turned out I had a B−. Still, not bad. In Strahl's class a B− was practically an A. I looked around discreetly to see who was celebrating having gotten an A as the papers were passed back. But nobody showed any sign of celebrating. Not Lukas or Kevin or any of the other math wizards. Instead, Strahl held on to one assignment, walked it personally to the back row, and handed it to Tschichatschow. Tschick was sitting there chewing intently on strong peppermint gum. He didn't look at Strahl. He just stopped chewing and breathing. Strahl bent down, wet his lips, and said, "Andrej."

There was practically no reaction. His head turned ever so slightly — like in a gangster film when somebody hears the click of the hammer when a gun is put to his head.

"Your assignment. I don't know what it is," said Strahl, leaning a hand on Tschick's desk. "I mean, if you didn't have this at your old school, you'll have to repeat math class. You didn't even . . . you don't seem to have even attempted to solve the problems. All the stuff written here" — Strahl leafed through the pages of Tschick's assignment and lowered his voice, though you could still hear him fine — "these *jokes*. I mean, if you haven't studied it before, I'll take that into account, of course. I had to give you an F, but the grade is, shall we say, not written in stone. I would suggest that you turn to Kevin or Lukas. Have a look at their assignments. Go over their notes from the last two months. Ask them any questions you have. Because the way things are going now, there's just no point."

Tschick nodded. He nodded in a very understanding kind of way, and then it happened. He fell off his chair, right at Strahl's feet. Strahl flinched and Patrick and Julia jumped up. Tschick lay on the floor as if he were dead.

We all figured the Russian was capable of a lot of things, but passing out because he was so sensitive about getting an F on his math homework was not one of them. But as it turned out, it had nothing to do with any sensitivity on his part. He hadn't eaten anything all morning and had obviously drunk a lot of alcohol. In the school nurse's office he filled the sink with puke and then was sent home.

Still, it didn't help his reputation much. Nobody ever found out what the jokes were that he put in his notebook instead of the math problems, and I can't remember who ended up having the A. But what I do know and will probably never forget, is the look on Strahl's face when the Russian keeled over at his feet. Holy crap.

The annoying thing about the whole story, however, wasn't that Tschick fell out of his seat or that he got an F. The annoying thing was that two weeks later he got a B. And then an E after that. And then another B. Strahl was going bananas. He said things like, "Your studying paid off," and "Don't let up now," but even a blind person could see that his Bs had nothing to do with whether he was studying or not. All it had to do with was whether he was drunk or not.

This slowly dawned on the teachers as well, and Tschick was reprimanded and sent home a few times. There were discussions with him behind closed doors too, but the school didn't do much about it at first. Tschick had had a difficult time in life or whatever, and in the wake of recent education system scandals everyone wanted to prove that even a low-class, drunken Russian would be given a fair shake in the German school system. So there were no real consequences. And after a while, the situation got calmer. Nobody knew what had been bothering Tschick, but after a while he got by okay in most subjects. He chewed less and less peppermint gum in class. And he didn't create any disturbances. If it wasn't for his occasional bender, you might even have forgotten he was there.

*"A man who has not seen Herr K. in a long time greeted him
with the words, 'You haven't changed at all.' 'Oh,' said Herr
K., turning pale.* Now that was an agreeably short story."

Mr. Kaltwasser took off his jacket as he walked in and
threw it over the back of his chair. Kaltwasser was our German
teacher, and he always entered the class without saying hello.
Or at least, you never heard a greeting because he started the
lesson before he even walked in the door. I have to admit that
I didn't really know what to make of Kaltwasser. Besides
Wagenbach, Kaltwasser was the only other staff member who
actually did a decent job of teaching. But while Wagenbach
was an asshole — as a person — you couldn't really tell what
Kaltwasser was like. I couldn't, anyway. He came in like a
machine and just started talking. That went on for precisely
forty-five minutes. And then Kaltwasser left again. You never
had any idea what to think of him. I couldn't say what he was
like as a person. I couldn't even say whether I thought he
was nice or not. Everyone else seemed to think he was about as
nice as a frozen turd, but I'm not so sure. I could imagine that,
outside school, he might be okay in his own way.

"Agreeably short," Kaltwasser repeated. "And I'm sure some of you thought you could keep an interpretation of the story just as brief. But of course it's not that simple. Or did someone here find it that simple? Who would like to begin? Volunteers? Come on, people. The back row seems to be catching my eye."

We turned and followed Kaltwasser's glance to the back row. Tschick had his head on the desk and you couldn't tell whether he was looking at his book or sleeping. It was sixth period.

"May I be so bold as to disturb you, Mr. Tschichatschow?"

"What?" Tschick's head rose slowly. The ironic formality of Kaltwasser's question set off alarm bells.

"Are you there, Mr. Tschichatschow?"

"On the job."

"Did you do your homework assignment?"

"Of course."

"Would you be so kind as to read it to us?"

"Uh, okay." Tschick looked quickly around, spotted his bag on the floor, plunked it down on his desk, and began looking for his notebook. As always, he hadn't unpacked his things at the beginning of the period. He kept pulling more and more notebooks out and seemed to be putting real effort into finding the right one.

"If you didn't do the assignment, just say so."

"I have the assignment — where is it? Where is it?" He put a notebook down on his desk, shoved the rest back into his bag, and started paging through the one on his desk. "Here it is. Shall I read it?"

"I insist."

"Right, I'll get started. The assignment was the *Stories of Herr K*. Here we go. Interpretation of the *Stories of Herr K*. The first question you have, of course, when you read Precht's stories . . ."

"Brecht," said Kaltwasser. "Bertolt Brecht."

"Aha." Tschick fished a ballpoint pen out of his bag and scribbled in his notebook. He put the pen back in the bag.

"Interpretation of the *Stories of Herr K*. The first question you have, of course, is who this mysterious person behind the letter *K* might be. Without overstating things, it's possible to say that it is a man who avoids the spotlight. He hides behind a letter — the letter *K*. It is the eleventh letter of the alphabet. Why is he hiding? Because in actuality, Herr K. is a weapons dealer. Along with other murky figures (Herr L. and Herr F.), he founded a criminal organization that considers the Geneva Convention a joke. He's sold tanks and fighter jets and made billions, but nowadays avoids getting involved in the actual dirty work. Instead, he cruises the Mediterranean on his yacht, where the CIA came after him. So Herr K. fled to South America and had his face altered by the renowned plastic surgeon Dr. M. And now he is taken aback that someone has recognized him and thus turns pale. It goes without saying that both the man who has recognized him on the street and the renowned plastic surgeon will soon find themselves in very deep water wearing cement shoes. That's it."

I looked at Tatiana. Her brow was furrowed and she had a pencil in her mouth. Then I looked at Kaltwasser. There was nothing to read in his face. Kaltwasser seemed to be tense, but more the kind of tension you show when you're interested in something. Nothing more. He didn't give Tschick a grade. Next Anja read the proper interpretation, the one that Google gives. Then there was a long discussion about whether Brecht was a communist. And then the period was over. All this happened shortly before summer break.

Now I have to talk about Tatiana's birthday. Tatiana's birthday fell during summer break, and there was going to be a
huge party. Tatiana had announced the party way in advance.
Word was that she was going to celebrate her fourteenth birthday out in Werder, near Potsdam, just southwest of Berlin, and
that everyone would be invited to stay overnight and everything. She asked all her best friends about their schedules
because she wanted to make sure they'd be able to come. And
since Natalie was leaving for the summer on the third day of
break, the whole thing had to be pushed forward to the second
day of summer break. Which is why all the details came out so
early.

The house in Werder belonged to an uncle of Tatiana's and
was right on a lake. The uncle was willing to basically hand it
over to Tatiana, and there wouldn't be any other adults around
except for him. The party was going to go all night and
everyone was supposed to bring their sleeping bags.

Obviously it was a big topic of conversation in class, for
weeks in advance. I kept thinking about the uncle. I'm not sure
why I found him so fascinating, but I figured he must have
been a pretty interesting guy — I mean, he was willing to hand

over his house for a party, not to mention that he was related to Tatiana. Anyway, I was excited to meet him. I pictured myself talking to him in the living room, standing next to the fireplace, having a great conversation. Though I didn't even know if there was a fireplace in the house. I wasn't the only one excited about the party. Julia and Natalie had been thinking for ages about what they were going to give Tatiana — you could read that in the notes they passed to each other in class. That is, I could read it because I sat in a chair that was in the direct line between the two of them and had to pass the notes. I was electrified by their gift ideas, and couldn't think about anything except what I could give Tatiana for her birthday. Julia and Natalie had finally decided to give her the new Beyoncé CD. Natalie had to check something from a list Julia made that looked something like this:

- *Beyoncé*
- *P!nk*
- *the necklace with the [illegible]*
- *make a list with more suggestions*

Natalie put a check next to the top item. Everybody knew Tatiana loved Beyoncé. Which at first was a bit of a problem for me, because I always thought Beyoncé was shit. At least musically. She looked great, of course, and actually there was definitely some similarity between the way she looked and the way Tatiana looked. So after a while, I didn't think Beyoncé was so shit after all. On the contrary. I began to like Beyoncé. I even liked her music suddenly. No, wait, that's not right. I thought her music was *fantastic*. I bought her last two albums and listened to them nonstop while thinking of Tatiana and wondering what I was going to show up at her party with to give her for her birthday. There was no way I could give her a Beyoncé album. Julia and Natalie and probably thirty others had already come up with that idea — Tatiana was going to get thirty Beyoncé CDs and would have to exchange twenty-nine of them. I wanted to give her something special but couldn't think of anything. Until that note with the multiple choice question crossed my desk.

I went to the store and bought an expensive fashion magazine with Beyoncé's face on the cover and started sketching it. Using a ruler, I drew evenly spaced lines vertically and horizontally across the photo until the whole thing was divided up into little squares. Then I took out a huge piece of paper and penciled in a set of squares five times larger than those on the magazine cover. I learned this method from a book. *The Old Masters* or something like that. You can use the method to make a large picture based on a small one. You just recreate it square by square. You could do it on a copy machine too. But I wanted it to be a drawing. I guess I wanted people to be able to see that I put real effort into it. If you show a lot of effort, people can figure out the rest. I worked on the drawing every day for weeks. I worked really hard. With just a pencil. And I just got more and more worked up while working on the drawing, thinking about Tatiana and her party and the supercool uncle I was going to have such a witty conversation with next to the fireplace.

There may be a lot of things I'm no good at, but drawing isn't one of them. It's like the high jump. If drawing Beyoncé and doing the high jump were the most important disciplines in the world, I would be way ahead. Seriously. But unfortunately nobody gives a damn about the high jump, and as for drawing I was beginning to have my doubts. After four weeks of hard work, Beyoncé looked almost like a photo — a giant pencil Beyoncé with Tatiana's eyes — and I probably would have been the happiest person in the universe, if only I had then gotten an invitation to Tatiana's party. But I didn't get one.

It was the last day of school, and I was a little nervous because the classroom was bursting with thoughts of the party. Everyone was talking nonstop about Werder, but no invitations had been passed out. At least I hadn't seen any. Nobody knew exactly where the party house was, and Werder isn't so tiny that you couldn't miss it. I had already memorized the map of Werder. I figured Tatiana would tell everyone the address on the last day of school. But that's not what happened.

Instead, two rows in front of me, I spotted a small green card in Arndt's pencil case. It was during math. I saw Arndt show the little card to Kallenbach, who frowned. I could see there was a little map in the middle of the card. And then I looked around and realized everyone had these green cards. Almost everyone. Kallenbach didn't have one, given the way he was staring at Arndt's like an idiot. Though he always looked liked an idiot. He was an idiot. That's probably why he wasn't invited. Kallenbach bent down to look closely at the writing on the card — he was nearsighted but for whatever reason never wore his glasses. Then Arndt pulled it away from him and shoved it into his bag. As I figured out later, Kallenbach and I weren't the only ones who didn't get invitations. The Nazi didn't get one, Tschichatschow didn't get one, and neither did one or two others. Of course. Boring kids and losers weren't invited — Russians, Nazis, and idiots. I didn't have to think for long to figure out what Tatiana thought of me. Because I wasn't a Russian or a Nazi.

Otherwise pretty much the entire class was invited, along with people from some of the other classes. Probably a hundred people. But I wasn't invited.

I kept hoping right until the last period of the day and the distribution of our final report cards. I hoped that it was all a mistake and that when the final bell rang Tatiana would come over to me and say, "Psycho, man, I forgot to give you one of these! Here's the invite! I hope you can make it — I'd be terribly disappointed if you, of all people, weren't able to come. Have you thought about what you're giving me for a present? Of course, I can depend on you! Okay, see you there. I really hope you can make it! My God, I can't believe I almost forgot to give you one!" Then the bell rang and everyone went home. I packed up my things slowly, to give Tatiana every opportunity to realize her mistake.

Out in the hall, the only people still standing around were the fat kids and nerds, all talking about their grades and crap like that. As I walked out of the building, maybe twenty meters from the door, someone grabbed my shoulder and said, "Awesome jacket." It was Tschick. His eyes were narrowed even more than usual as he smiled, and I saw both rows of his teeth. "I'll buy it. The jacket. Hold up a minute."

I didn't stop, but I could hear that he was still following me.

"It's my favorite," I said. "Not for sale." I'd found it at a thrift shop and bought it for five Euros, and it really was my favorite jacket. Made in China, with a white dragon printed on the chest. Supercheap-looking, but also supercool. The perfect jacket for a low-class tough. Which is why I liked it so much — at first glance you couldn't tell that I was exactly the opposite of a low-class tough: a rich scaredy-cat totally unable to defend himself.

"Where can I get one? Hey, wait up! Where are you going?" He shouted across the entire parking lot and thought it was funny. It sounded as if he'd had more than just alcohol. I turned onto a side street.

"Did you get held back?" he continued.

"What are you shouting about?"

"Did you fail?"

"No."

"You look like you were failed."

"What do you mean?"

"You look like you just found out you got held back, that you'll have to repeat."

What did he want from me? I caught myself thinking that Tatiana had made a good decision not to invite him.

"Bunch of Ds, though, eh?"

"No idea."

"What do you mean, 'No idea'? If I'm bothering you, just say the word."

I was supposed to tell him he was bothering me? And then he'd punch me in the face, or what?

"I don't know."

"You don't know if I'm bothering you?"

"No, whether I got a bunch of Ds."

"Seriously?"

"I didn't look yet."

"At your report card?"

"Nope."

"You didn't look at your report card yet?"

"Nope."

"Really? You got your report card and didn't even look at it? How cool is that?" He was gesturing wildly as he talked, and as he walked next to me I realized he wasn't actually any taller than me. Just more stocky.

"So you won't sell me the jacket?"

"No."

"What are you up to now?"

"Going home."

"And then?"

"Nothing."

"And after that?"

"None of your damn business." Now that I realized he wasn't going to mug me, I felt braver. That's the way it always is, unfortunately. When somebody is hostile to me, I'm so nervous that I can barely keep my knees from buckling. But if they are even the slightest bit friendly, I immediately start insulting them.

He walked silently beside me for another hundred meters or so, then tugged on my sleeve and said again what a cool jacket he thought it was. Then he slipped through some bushes along the side of the road. I watched him trudge off across the grassy wasteland in the direction of the high-rise apartment blocks, with the plastic grocery bag he used as his school knapsack hanging over his right shoulder.

CHAPTER THIRTEEN

After a while I stopped and sat down on the curb. I didn't feel like going home. I didn't want it to turn into just another day. It was a special day. An especially crappy day. I took forever getting home.

When I opened the door, nobody was there. A note was on the table: *Dinner's in the fridge*. I unpacked my things, looked at my report card, put on the Beyoncé CD, and crawled under my blanket. I couldn't decide whether the music comforted me or made me even more depressed. I think, actually, it depressed me even more.

A few hours later I went back to school to pick up my bike. I'd forgotten it. Seriously. It was about two kilometers to my school, and some days I walked. But I hadn't walked that day. I'd been so deep in thought when Tschick started talking to me that I had unlocked and then relocked my bike, and then just marched off. It really was a horrible day.

So I followed the route for the third time of the day, past the piles of dirt and the playground at the edge of the wasteland. I climbed up the lookout tower of the play fort and sat down. It was a wooden tower with a fence built partway around it so little kids could play cowboys and Indians. If there'd been any little kids around. But I'd never seen a little kid there. Or even an older kid or adult for that matter. Not even junkies slept there. I was the only one ever there, sitting up in the tower when I felt crappy, where nobody could see me. To the east you could see the high-rises of Hellersdorf. To the north, Weiden Lane wandered off beyond the bushes, and farther on was a colony of little summer cabins. But around the playground was absolutely nothing, just a wide open wasteland that had originally been a construction site. It was supposed to have been the site of a brand-new town house development — you could still see a description of the development on the big weather-beaten sign that had fallen over on the side of the street. COMING SOON: 96 BEAUTIFUL NEW TOWN HOUSES. Below that was something about what lucrative investments they'd make, and somewhere at the bottom it said KLINGENBERG REAL ESTATE & DEVELOPMENT.

But one day they'd found three extinct bugs, a frog, and a rare grasshopper, and ever since the environmentalists have been suing the developers and the developers have been suing the environmentalists and the lot has been left empty. The court battle has gone on for ten years now, and if my father is to be believed, it'll take another ten years to be settled — because there's no way to beat the environmental fascists. That's my father's term: "environmental fascists." And these days he drops the word "environmental" from the phrase too, because the court battle has ruined him. A quarter of the land in the development site belonged to him, and all the suits and countersuits landed him right in the toilet. If an outsider were to listen to our dinner table conversation sometime, he wouldn't understand a single word. For years, all my father has talked about is shit, assholes, and fascists. For a long time I wasn't sure how much he'd lost and how it would affect us. I always thought my father would figure a way to get out of the whole thing with some legal loophole — and maybe he thought so too. At least at first. But then he'd thrown in the towel and sold his share. He took a huge loss, but he figured the loss would be even bigger if he kept going back to court with the rest of the developers. So he sold his share in the project to the assholes. That's what he calls the people he worked with. The assholes continued to fight in court for the right to build. That was a year and a half ago. And for a year now, it's been clear: That was the beginning of the end. My father tried to make up for the losses on the Weiden Lane development by playing the stock market, and now we're broke, our vacation's off, and the house we own doesn't belong to us anymore. That's what my father says. And all because of three caterpillars and a grasshopper.

The only thing left of the development is the playground, which was built at the very beginning to demonstrate how child-friendly the area was. But it was all for nothing.

I'll also admit there was another reason I hung around that playground. From up there on top of the tower you could see two white apartment buildings. The buildings are behind the colony of summer cabins, somewhere beyond the woods. And Tatiana lives in one of them. I never knew where exactly, but there's a window at the top of the building on the left where you can see a green light whenever the sun starts to go down. For whatever reason, I just decided that was where she lived. So sometimes I just sit on the lookout tower and wait until I see that green light go on. When I'm on the way from soccer practice or an afterschool class. I peer through the cracks between the boards and carve letters in the wood with my keys — if the green light comes on I get a warm feeling in my heart, and if it doesn't, it's always a huge disappointment.

But that day it was much too early, so instead of waiting I headed back toward school. My bike was there, lonely and alone in the bike stand that looked as if it stretched for miles. The flag was hanging limp on the flagpole, and there was nobody left in the building. The only person around was the janitor, who I saw pulling two trash cans out to the street. A convertible blasting Turkish hip-hop steamed past. This is how the place would be for the rest of the summer. No school for six weeks. No Tatiana for six weeks. I pictured myself hanging from the playground lookout tower by a rope.

Back home I didn't know what to do. I tried to fix the headlight on my bike, which had been broken for a long time. But I didn't have the replacement part I needed. I put on *Survivor* by Destiny's Child and started rearranging the furniture in my room. I pushed the bed to the front of the room and the desk to the back. Then I went back downstairs and fiddled around some more with the bike light. But it was pointless, so I tossed my tools in the flower garden, went back upstairs, threw myself onto the bed, and started screaming. It was the first day of summer vacation and I was already going crazy. At some point I pulled out the drawing of Beyoncé. I looked at it for a long time, then held it up in front of me with two hands and began to tear it in half, very slowly. When I'd ripped it as far as Beyoncé's forehead, I stopped. That's when I started to cry. And what happened after that I can no longer remember. All I know is that at some stage I dashed out of the house and into the woods and up a hill, and then I started to run. You couldn't really say I was going for a run because I was wearing normal clothes, but I did pass about twenty runners per minute on the trails through the woods. I just ran through the trees screaming, and I was incredibly pissed off at everyone else who was running in the woods because they could *hear* me. When I saw a guy walking with ski poles coming toward me, I could barely keep myself from grabbing his stupid poles and beating his ass with them.

When I got home again I stood in the shower for hours. I felt a bit better afterward — like somebody who's been floating around the Atlantic in a lifeboat for weeks and finally sights a ship only to have the ship come alongside and toss him a can of Red Bull and keep on going. That's about how I felt.

Downstairs I heard the front door open.

"What's all that stuff lying around outside?" yelled my father.

I tried to ignore him, but it was difficult.

"Do you plan on leaving it there?"

He meant the tools I'd been working on my bicycle with. After checking in the mirror to see if my eyes were still red, I headed downstairs again. When I got outside there was a taxi driver standing in front of the house scratching his crotch.

"Go up and tell you mother it's time to go," said my father. "Have you even said good-bye? You forgot, didn't you? Go on upstairs! Go!"

He hustled me up the stairs. I was pissed. But unfortunately my father was right. I'd completely forgotten about the whole thing with my mother. I'd known for the past few days, but somehow in all the excitement I'd forgotten. My mother had to go off again to rehab for a month.

She was sitting in a fur coat in front of the mirror in their bedroom, and she was tanked. There wouldn't be anything available at rehab, after all. I helped her up and carried her suitcase down. My father carried the suitcase to the taxi, and the taxi had barely pulled away before he called her — as if he was terribly worried about her. But that wasn't the case, as soon would be clear. My mother hadn't been gone for half an hour before my father came into my room with a clownishly somber face on, and in a clownishly somber voice said, "I'm your father. And we need to talk about something serious. Something that won't be pleasant for you or for me."

It was the same face he put on a few years earlier when he said he needed to talk to me about sex. It was the same face he put on when he told me that because of some sort of cat allergy, we had to put not only our cats but also my turtle and the two rabbits I kept in the garden to sleep. That was the face he looked at me with now.

"I just found out I have a business meeting," he said, as if he himself was baffled by the whole thing. He grimaced for extra effect. He babbled on a bit more, but the upshot was simple. He was going to leave me alone for fourteen days.

I made a face meant to signal that I needed to put in some very serious thought about whether I'd be able to handle such a tragic situation. Could I handle it? Fourteen days all alone in a cruel air-conditioned world consisting only of swimming in our pool, eating delivery pizzas, and watching videos projected on the wall? Yes, I nodded sorrowfully, I could give it a try, and yes, I'd probably survive somehow.

His furrowed brow and downward-turned mouth relaxed a little. I guess I overdid it.

"And don't you dare get yourself into any stupid shit! Don't think you can misbehave. I'm going to leave two hundred Euros — it's already downstairs on the table, and if there's any problem, call me immediately."

"At your *business* meeting."

"That's right, at my *business meeting*." He looked at me angrily.

He made another call to my mother, pretending he was worried, and while he was on the phone his assistant arrived to pick him up. I went straight downstairs to see whether it was still the same one. Because she's extremely hot, and only a few years older than me — probably nineteen or so. And she always laughs. It's almost unbelievable how much she laughs. I had met her for the first time about two years earlier when I visited my father at his office. And she had run her fingers through my hair and laughed when I used the copy machine to make images of the right and left sides of my face, my hands, and my bare feet. She doesn't do that anymore, unfortunately. Run her fingers through my hair, I mean.

She hopped out of the car wearing shorts and a skintight sweater, and it was immediately clear what sort of business meeting this was going to be. The sweater was so tight you could see every detail. I decided it was okay that my father hadn't bothered to put on a big show of hiding the whole thing. He didn't need to. Both of my parents knew the score. My mother knew what my father was up to, and my father knew what my mother was up to. And when they were alone together, they screamed at each other.

The thing I didn't understand for a long time was why they didn't just get separated. For a while I thought I was the reason.

Or money was the reason. But eventually I decided they actually liked screaming at each other. That they liked being unhappy. I read about it in a magazine somewhere — that there were people who liked being unhappy. People who were actually happy when they were unhappy. Though I have to admit that I didn't entirely understand the article. I mean, on the one hand a light went on in my head, but on the other I didn't really get it.

Still, I've never come up with a better explanation for the way my parents are. And I've thought about it a lot. So much sometimes that I get a headache thinking about it. It's like when you look at those 3-D pictures, where you have to stare at a pattern until an invisible shape pops out. Other people were always better at that than I was — with me, I could barely get it to work at all. And as soon as I was able to see the invisible shape — usually a flower or a deer or whatever — it disappeared again immediately and I'd get a headache. That's exactly how it is when I try to figure out what the deal is with my parents: I just get a headache. So I don't think about it anymore.

While my father packed his suitcase upstairs, I made conversation with Mona downstairs. That's her name, Mona. The assistant. The first thing she said to me was how warm it was and how it was supposed to get even warmer in the next few days. The usual. But when she heard I'd have to spend my summer vacation alone, she looked at me with such a sad face that my own tragic fate nearly brought tears to my eyes. Abandoned by my parents, God, and the world! I thought about asking her to run her fingers through my hair again like she had next to the copier that time. But I was too shy to ask. Instead, I stared the whole time at her skintight sweater while pretending to be looking past her and studying the landscape, out the window, as she jabbered on about what a highly responsible man my father was, blah, blah, blah. Getting older had its pluses and its minuses.

I was deeply engrossed in studying the landscape when my father came down the stairs with his suitcase.

"Don't feel sorry for him," he said. He gave me the same warnings he had given me before, told me for the third time where he had left the two hundred Euros, then put his arm around Mona's waist and walked out with her to the car. He could have spared me that. Putting his arm around her, I mean. I think it's fine that they don't put on some sort of show of secrecy, but he could at least wait to put his arm around her until they're off our property. That's my opinion. I slammed the door, closed my eyes, and stood there silent and still for a minute. Then I threw myself down onto the tile floor and started to sob.

"Mona!" I cried. My throat tightened. "I have to confess something to you!" My voice echoed ominously in the empty foyer, and Mona, who already seemed to have sensed that I needed to confess something to her, put her hands to her mouth in horror.

"Oh, God, oh, God!" she cried.

"You can't take this the wrong way," I sobbed. "I'd never work for the CIA voluntarily! But they've got us by the throat — do you understand?" Of course she understood. She collapsed next to me, crying.

"But what are we supposed to do?" she cried frantically.

"There's nothing we can do!" I answered. "We just have to play along with their game. The most important thing is to keep up the façade. You have to keep reminding yourself that I'm an *eighth grader*, and that I *look* like an eighth grader, and that we have to live our lives as if everything's normal — we have to pretend for another year or two that we don't even know each other!"

"Oh, God, oh, God!" cried Mona, throwing her arms around my neck. "How could I ever doubt you?"

"Oh, God, oh, God!" I cried, pressing my forehead onto the cold tile floor and doubling over. I cried on the floor for about half an hour. And after that I felt better.

CHAPTER
FOURTEEN

I cried until the Vietnamese woman showed up. She normally comes three times a week. The Vietnamese woman is pretty old — about sixty, I guess — and can't really speak German. Without a word, she shuffled past me into the kitchen and came back out with the vacuum cleaner. I watched her working for a while; then I went over to her and told her that she didn't need to work the next two weeks. I wanted to be alone. I told her that my parents would be away during that time, and that if she just came by two weeks from Tuesday and whipped things into shape, that would be great. It was tough to put it in a way that she understood. I thought she'd drop the vacuum out of pure joy, but that's not what happened at all. At first she didn't believe me. So I showed her the list of chores my father had left for me to do, and all the things he'd stocked up on for me, and then I showed her the calendar where my father had circled in red the Wednesday he'd be back. But she still didn't believe me, so I showed her the two hundred Euros he had left. And that's when I realized why she was so stubbornly clinging to her vacuum cleaner. Because she thought she wouldn't get paid if she didn't work. So then I had to explain that she'd get paid anyway. Man, I was so embarrassed. Nobody will notice, I told her. It took a lot of effort to get it across to her because she doesn't speak German. But at some point she did leave — after we'd gone back to the calendar and both pointed several times at the Tuesday in two weeks and looked in each other's eyes and nodded. I was worn out by the time she left. I never know what to say in these situations. We had an Indian working as a gardener for a while too, though he was let go to save money. But it was the same with him. It's so embarrassing. I want to treat them like regular people, but they act like they're servants who are there just to move the dirt out of your way — which, granted, is why they're there. But I'm only four-teen! My parents don't have a problem with it. And if they are around it's no problem for me either. But when I'm alone in a room with the Vietnamese woman I feel like Hitler. I always want to grab the rags out of her hand and clean everything up myself.

I walked her out, and I would like to have given her some-thing too. But I didn't know what. So I just waved like an idiot as she walked off, and was incredibly relieved once I was finally alone again. I gathered up the tools that were still lying in the flower garden and then stood there in the warm evening air and took a few nice deep breaths.

Diagonally across the street the Dyckerhoffs were barbe-cuing. The oldest son waved with the grill tongs in his hand. Like all our neighbors he's an incredible asshole, so I quickly looked away. And that's when I saw a creaky bicycle cruising down the street. Though cruising down the street is overstat-ing it a bit. And to call it a bicycle is also a stretch. It was the frame of an old girls' bike, but it had two different-sized wheels in the front and back. In the middle was a tattered old leather seat. There was also a hand brake dangling down from the handlebars. It looked like a broken antenna. The back tire was flat. And riding the contraption was Tschichatschow. With the exception of my father, he was pretty much the last person I wanted to run into right then. Though to be honest, other than Tatiana, everyone was the last person I wanted to run into. But the expression on his Mongolian-looking face told me he didn't feel the same way.

"*Kablam!*" Tschick said, smiling as he steered his bike onto the sidewalk in front of me. "You know what happened? I was riding over there — and *kablam*. This is where you live? Hey, is that a flat-tire repair kit? How cool is that! Can I use it?"

I didn't feel like talking. I gave him all the tools and told him just to leave them there when he was done. I was busy, I said, I had to get going. Then I went straight inside and listened through the closed door to see if he was maybe going to take off with the tools. After a little while I went upstairs, lay down in my room, and tried to think about something else. But it wasn't so easy. I could hear the clang of the tools downstairs as he tinkered with his bike. He was singing in Russian too. Really badly. And somebody in the neighborhood was mowing their lawn. But when things finally quieted down around the house, it made me uneasy. I looked out the window and saw somebody walking around our backyard. Tschick walked all the way around the pool, then stood shaking his head in amazement next to the aluminum ladder while scratching his back with a screwdriver he was carrying. I opened the window.

"Awesome pool!" yelled Tschick, smiling up at me.

"Yeah, awesome pool, awesome jacket. Now what?"

He just stood there. So I went downstairs and we chatted a little. Tschick couldn't get over the pool. He wanted to know what my father did, so I told him. I wanted to know what he'd said to get the Ford Fiesta dude to stop bothering him. He shrugged his shoulders. "Russian mafia." He grinned. And I could tell that wasn't the real answer. But he wouldn't tell me what he'd really said, despite my pestering him for a while. We talked about this and that and eventually — inevitably — we made our way over to the PlayStation and started playing *GTA*. Tschick didn't know how, and we didn't get far. But still, this was better than lying in the corner and screaming.

"And you really didn't get held back?" he asked at some point. "I mean, did you end up looking at your report card? I still don't get that. Man, you're on vacation, you'll probably go somewhere cool with your parents, you can go to that party, you've got an awesome . . ."

"What party?"

"Aren't you going to Tatiana's?"

"Nah, don't feel like it."

"Seriously?"

"I have other plans for tomorrow," I said, pushing madly on the triangle button of the game controller. "And besides, I'm not invited."

"You didn't get invited? That sucks. I thought I was the only one."

"It'll be boring anyway," I said, running over a few people with a tanker truck.

"Maybe if you're gay. But for a guy like me that party is the ultimate. Simla will be there. And Natalie. And Laura and

Corinna and Sarah. Not to mention Tatiana. And Mia. And Fadile and Cathy and Kimberley. And sweet-ass Jennifer. And that blonde from the other class. And her sister. And Melanie."

"Huh," I said, staring blankly at the TV screen. Tschick was staring blankly at the screen too.

"Let me try the helicopter," he said.

I handed him the controller and we didn't talk any more about the party.

When Tschick headed home, it was almost midnight. I heard the bike creak off toward Weiden Lane, and then stood alone in front of our house for a minute. Above, stars in the night sky. And that was the best thing about the entire day: that it was finally over.

Things were better the next morning. I woke up as early as I normally did for school. Couldn't change my inner alarm clock that quickly. But the silence in the house reminded me: I'm all alone and it's summer break, the place belongs to me, and I can do whatever I feel like.

The first thing I did was carry some CDs downstairs and crank the stereo in the living room all the way up. I put on the White Stripes. Then I opened the back door and lay down by the pool with three bags of chips, a Coke, and my favorite book and tried to put all the bad shit out of my mind.

Even though it was still early, it was already ninety degrees in the shade. I dangled my feet in the water, and Count Luckner began to talk to me. That's my favorite book: *Count Luckner, The Sea Devil*. I've already read it at least three times, but I figured another time couldn't hurt. Count Luckner is a pirate during World War I and sinks one English ship after another. But he does it in a gentlemanly way. Meaning he doesn't kill anyone. He scuttles their ships but saves all the crewmen and takes them ashore, all in the service of His Majesty, the Kaiser. And the book's not made up, it all really happened. The coolest part is when he's in Australia. He works as a lighthouse keeper and a kangaroo hunter. I mean, he was *fifteen*. He didn't know a soul down there. He jumped ship, joined the Salvation Army, then ended up working at the lighthouse and hunting kangaroos. But I haven't gotten that far yet this time through.

The sun was beating down, so I opened up the patio umbrella. The wind blew it over. So I put it upright again and laid some heavy things on the base. Then everything was peaceful. But I couldn't read. I was suddenly so excited about the idea that I could do anything I wanted that I did nothing at all. I'm completely different from Count Luckner in that regard. I sat back and went through all the crap with Tatiana again in my mind. Then I realized that the lawn needed to be watered. My father had forgotten to tell me to do it, so I could have gotten away with not doing it. But I did it anyway. It would have bugged me if I had to do it, but now that the house basically belonged to me and the yard was *my* yard, I kind of enjoyed watering the lawn. I stood on the steps in front of the house and sprayed with the hose. I had cranked the faucet all the way open and the water must have shot fifty meters through the air. Still, I couldn't reach the farthest corner of the front yard, despite my trying out all kinds of tricks and messing with the nozzle. Because I had to do it without leaving the front stoop. I'd made that a rule. The White Stripes were cranked up in the living room, the door was open, and there I stood, barefoot, with my pants rolled up and a pair of sunglasses on top of my head, the lord of the manor spraying his acreage. And I could do this every morning! I didn't really want to be seen doing it, but I didn't see anybody around. It was 8:30 on the second day of vacation, and everybody was sleeping in. Two blue tits chirped in the yard. The pleasantly pensive and recently fallen-in-love Lord von Klingenberg tarried all alone, surveying his estate. Well, not entirely alone. Jack and Meg were visiting, as they often did when they were looking to get away from the constant crush of paparazzi, and putting on a little jam session in the back room. The lord of the manor would soon join them and play along to a few rocking tunes on his recorder. The birds chirped, the water rained down on the grass . . . nothing pleased Lord von Klingenberg more than these mornings filled with birdsong as he watered his lawn. He crimped the hose, waited ten seconds for the pressure to build up, then shot a sixty meter surface to surface missile of water at the rhododendrons. *In the cold, cold night*, sang Meg White.

A rickety car came limping down the street. It was a Lada, a small Russian car shaped a little like a jeep. It slowed in front of our house and pulled into the driveway. For a minute, the light blue Lada stood in front of our garage with the engine still running. Then it shut off. The driver's side door opened and Tschick got out. He put his elbows on the roof and watched me spraying the lawn.

"Huh," he said. Then he was silent for a while. "Is that fun?"

I kept waiting for his father or his brother or somebody else to get out of the car, but nobody else appeared. And the reason was that nobody else was in the car. It was just tough to see that through the dirty windows.

"You look like some kind of queer, or like you just discovered that somebody shat in your garden last night. You want me to drive you somewhere, or would you prefer to just keep sprinkling water around?" He smiled his broad Russian grin. "Hop in, man."

Obviously I didn't get in. I wasn't completely crazy. I went over and sat down in the passenger seat, with my feet still out of the car. I didn't want to stand there all conspicuously in the driveway.

The Lada looked even worse inside than it did outside. There were a bunch of wires hanging out beneath the steering wheel, and a screwdriver was jammed up under the dashboard.

"Are you out of your mind?"

"I just borrowed it. It's not stolen," said Tschick. "I'll take it back. We've done it a million times."

"Who is *we*?"

"Me and my brother. He found it. It just sits on the street like garbage. You can borrow it. The owner never notices."

"What about all that?" I pointed to the jumble of wires.

"You can shove it back in."

"You're crazy. What about fingerprints?"

"Fingerprints? Is that why you're sitting so funny?" He pulled at my arm, which I had scrunched up against my chest. "Don't wet your pants. That's just police show bullshit. Fingerprints. Look, you can touch anything. Go ahead, touch whatever you want. Come on, let's take a spin."

"Not me." I looked at him and didn't say anything more at first. He really was crazy.

"Didn't you say yesterday that you wanted to get out and experience things?"

"By that I didn't mean prison."

"Prison? You're not criminally accountable — you're a minor."

"Do whatever you want. But I'm not going." To be honest, I had no idea how old you had to be to get charged as an adult. And I wasn't sure what "criminally accountable" meant. I mean, sort of. Basically. But not really.

"Nothing can happen to you. My brother always says to me that if he were my age, he'd rob a bank. They can't do anything to you until you're fifteen. My brother's thirty. In Russia, they beat the shit out of you anyway. But here! Nothing. And besides, nobody gives a crap about this car. Seriously. Not even the owner will miss it."

"No way."

"Just once around the block."

"No."

Tschick let up the emergency brake, and I can't really say why I didn't hop out. Normally I'm a scaredy-cat. Maybe for that reason I wanted not to be a scaredy-cat just once. With his left foot he stepped on the far left pedal, and the Lada rolled silently backward down the driveway. Then he stepped on the middle pedal with his right foot and the car stopped. Then he grabbed the wires hanging from the base of the steering wheel and the engine started. I closed my eyes. When I opened them again, we were gliding down Ketschendorf Way, and then we turned right into Rotraud Street.

"You didn't use your blinker," I said meekly, my arms still pressed to my chest. I was so nervous I thought I was going to keel over. Then I started grabbing for the seat belt.

"There's no reason to be scared. I drive like a champ."

"Put your blinker on like a champ."

"I've never blinked."

"Please."

"Why? Anyone can see where I'm turning. And there's nobody around anyway."

That was true. The street was empty. It remained true for about another minute. By then Tschick had turned twice more and we were on the Avenue of Cosmonauts. There are four lanes on the Avenue of Cosmonauts. I started to panic.

"Okay, okay. Let's go back now."

"I make Formula One drivers look like chumps."

"Yeah, you said that already."

"Isn't it true?"

"No."

"Seriously. Don't I drive well?" asked Tschick.

"Super," I said. And when it struck me that this was my mother's standard answer to my father's standard question, I added, "Just super, dear."

"Don't blow a gasket."

Tschick didn't drive like a Formula One champion, but he didn't drive too badly either. Not much better or worse than my father. And he had now started to head back in the direction of our neighborhood.

"Can't you follow the rules of the road? That's a double line you just crossed."

"Are you gay?"

"What?"

"I asked if you were gay."

"Have you lost your mind?"

"You called me *dear.*"

"I called you . . . what? That's called irony."

"Okay, so are you gay?"

"Because of my use of irony?"

"And because you're not interested in girls." He looked me directly in the eyes.

"Keep your eyes on the road!" I screamed. I have to admit I was getting a bit hysterical at this point. He was driving without even looking where he was going. My father did the same thing sometimes, but my father was my father and he had a driver's license.

"Everybody in the class is nuts for Tatiana. Absolutely nuts."

"Who?"

"Tatiana. There's a girl in our class named Tatiana. You never noticed her? Tatiana Superstar. You're the only one who never checks her out. So are you gay? I'm just asking."

I thought I was going to fall over and die.

"I don't have a problem with it," said Tschick. "I have an uncle in Moscow who runs around in leather pants with the ass cut out of them. He's totally cool otherwise. Works for the government. And he can't do anything about the fact that he's gay. There's really nothing wrong with it."

Holy crap. I mean, I don't have a problem with it if somebody's gay either. Though that's not how I pictured things in Russia — people running around in ass-less chaps. But that I acted like Tatiana Cosic didn't exist — that had to be a joke, right? Because *of course* I acted as if she didn't exist. How else could I act around her? For a complete nobody, a walking sleeping pill, that was the only way not to make a fool of myself in front of her.

"You're an idiot," I said.

"I'm cool with it. As long as you don't try to mess with my asshole."

"Cut it out. That's disgusting."

"My uncle . . ."

"Screw your uncle! I'm not gay, man. Can't you see I'm in a shitty mood?"

"Because I'm not putting my blinker on?"

"No, you idiot, because I'm not gay!"

Tschick looked at me, totally confused. He was silent. I didn't want to explain it. I hadn't meant to say a word about it, but it had slipped out. I'd never talked to anyone about something like this before, and I didn't want to start now.

"I don't understand," said Tschick. "Am I supposed to understand? You're in a shitty mood because you're not gay? Huh?"

I looked out the window, wounded. At least I didn't care when two old people stared at us through the dirty windows when we stopped next to them at a red light — they'd probably call the police. But at that point I hoped the police would pull us over. At least then there'd be some action.

"Okay, shitty mood . . . but why?"

"Because today is *the day*, man."

"What is today?"

"The party, idiot. Tatiana's party."

"You don't have to pretend now just because you're sexually disoriented. Yesterday you said you didn't want to go."

"As if I could."

"I really don't think there's anything wrong with it," said Tschick, putting a hand on my knee. "I don't give a crap about your sexuality problems, and I won't tell anyone, I swear."

"I can prove it," I said. "Shall I show you?"

"You want to show me that you're not gay? Oooo-kay," he said, swatting away invisible flies.

We were already close to home. This time Tschick didn't park in front of our house. He parked on a little side street, an alley where nobody would see us get out of the car. When we got upstairs and Tschick was still looking at me as if he'd found who knows what out about me, I said, "Don't blame me for what I'm about to show you. And don't laugh. If you laugh . . ."

"I won't laugh."

"You know Tatiana is crazy about Beyoncé, right?"

"Yeah, of course. I would have stolen a CD for her if she'd invited me to her party."

"Yeah. Anyway. Check this out."

I pulled the drawing out of a drawer. Tschick took it and held it up with his arms stretched out in front of him. At first he didn't pay as much attention to the drawing itself as to the backside, where I'd repaired the rip with clear tape so that you could barely see the rip from the front. He studied the rip and then looked at the drawing again. Then he said, "You have *feelings* for her."

He said it very seriously, without any crap. It was really strange. And it was the first time that I thought this guy wasn't so stupid after all. Tschick took one look at the rip and knew exactly what the story was. I don't know many people who could figure it out so quickly. Tschick looked at me with a solemn expression on his face. I liked that about him. He was somebody who could definitely play the fool. But when the chips were down, he didn't play around. He took things seriously.

"How long did this take you? Three months? It looks like a photo. What are you going to do with it now?"

"Nothing."

"You have to do something with it."

"What am I supposed to do with it? Am I supposed to go to Tatiana's and say, 'Hey, happy birthday, I have a little something for you here — and, oh, it doesn't bother me a bit that you didn't invite me even though you invited every other idiot, it's no problem, really. And it's actually just a coincidence that I was passing by. Anyway, hope you enjoy the drawing that I worked my ass off on for three months!'"

Tschick scratched his neck. He put the drawing on my desk, looked at it, shaking his head, then looked at me again and said, "That's exactly what I would do."

"Seriously, you have to do something. If you don't, you're crazy. Let's drive there. Who cares if you think it's embarrassing? Nothing is embarrassing in a stolen Lada. Put on your awesome jacket, grab your drawing, and get your ass into the car."

"Never."

"We'll wait until it's getting dark, and then you get your ass into the car."

"No."

"Why not?"

"I'm not invited."

"You're not invited! So what? I'm not invited either. And you know why? Because of course the Russian idiot doesn't get invited. But do you know why *you* weren't invited? See — you don't even know. But I do."

"Then say it, oh, Wise One: because I'm boring and ugly."

Tschick shook his head. "You're not ugly. Or maybe you are, I don't know. But that's got nothing to do with it. The reason is because there's no reason to invite you. You don't stand out. You have to get noticed, man."

"How am I supposed to stand out? Come to school drunk every day?"

"No. My God. But if I were you and looked like you and lived here and had clothes like yours, I'd have gotten a hundred invitations."

"Do you need clothes?"

"Don't change the subject. As soon as it gets dark, we're driving down there."

"No way."

"We're not going to go to the party. We're just going to drive past."

What an idiotic idea. Or, to be more precise, there were three ideas, and every single one of them was idiotic: show up without an invitation, drive a stolen Lada all the way across Berlin, and — craziest of all — take the drawing with us. Because one thing was clear: Tatiana would surely figure out the score when she saw the drawing. There was no way I was going.

While Tschick was driving me to Werder, the town where the party was, I kept muttering that I didn't want to go. At first I said that he should turn around, that I'd had a change of heart. Then I said that we didn't have the exact address. Then I swore that there was no way I would get out of the car when we arrived.

I kept my hands folded under my arms for the entire trip. This time it wasn't because I was afraid of leaving fingerprints but because I was shaking. Beyoncé was sitting on the dashboard in front of me and shaking too.

Despite my anxiety, I realized that Tschick was driving more carefully than he had earlier in the day. He avoided roads with multiple lanes and eased his foot off the gas as we approached red traffic lights so we wouldn't be sitting at any intersections letting people look into the car. At one point we had to pull over to the side of the road because there was a brief rain shower and the windshield wipers didn't work. But we were nearly out of the city by then. It poured, but only for five minutes. A passing thunderstorm. Afterward the air smelled fantastic.

As we started off again, I peered through the windshield and watched as the wind pushed the water droplets apart. It suddenly occurred to me how strange it was to be cruising in a car that didn't belong to us through the evening streets of the city, then along the tree-lined boulevards of West Berlin, past a lonely gas station, and then on little roads outside the city toward Werder. Eventually the red sun disappeared completely behind dark clouds. I didn't say another word, and Tschick was silent as well. And I was happy that he was so determined to get to the party that I supposedly didn't want to go to. I hadn't thought of anything else for three months — and now here it was and I was about to come across as the biggest loser ever, right in front of Tatiana.

It turned out the house wasn't hard to find. We probably could have found it if we'd just driven on the streets along the lake, but instead, as we passed the sign announcing we'd entered Werder, we spotted two kids on mountain bikes with sleeping bags strapped onto them — it was André and some other idiot. Tschick followed them but drove far enough behind them that they didn't notice. And then we saw the house. Redbrick, with a front yard full of bikes, and lots of noise coming from the backyard, which faced the lake. A hundred meters ahead of us. I slid down from my seat into the footwell as Tschick rolled down his window and hung his arm casually out of the car and drove past the scene at a snail's pace. There were about a dozen people in front of the house, standing around in the yard and in the open doorway — people with glasses and bottles in their hands, talking on phones, smoking cigarettes. There were loads more in the back. Familiar and unfamiliar faces, girls all tarted up. And like the sun, right in the middle, Tatiana. She may not have invited the biggest losers or the Russian, but she seemed to have invited everyone else with a pulse. We slowly passed the house. Nobody had seen us, and it occurred to me that I didn't have any idea how I was going to give the drawing to Tatiana. I began to think seriously about the idea of just tossing it out the window. Somebody would find it and take it to her. But before I could do something stupid, Tschick had stopped the car and hopped out. I watched him, horrified. I don't know if it's always so embarrassing to have a crush on somebody. Apparently I'm not very good at it. As I was debating whether to remain in the footwell and pull my jacket over my head or to get back into my seat and put an it-wasn't-my-idea look on my face, fireworks started going off behind the redbrick house, exploding red and yellow in the sky, and almost everyone ran into the backyard. The only people left out front were André and Tatiana, who'd come to say hi to him.

And Tschick.

Tschick was standing directly in front of them. They stared at him as if they didn't recognize him — and it's entirely possible they didn't recognize him. Because Tschick had my sunglasses on. And he was also wearing a pair of my jeans and my gray jacket. We'd spent the day going through my closet and I'd given Tschick three pairs of pants, a couple of shirts, a sweater, and a few other things. As a result he no longer looked like some hopeless Russian hardship case, but more like a soap opera star. And that's not meant to sound like an insult. But he just didn't look like himself anymore — he'd even put gel in his hair. I saw him start talking to Tatiana and saw her answer. She looked pissed. Tschick motioned to me behind his back. As if in a trance, I got out of the car and as for what happened next, don't ask me. I have no idea. I was suddenly next to Tatiana with the drawing in my hand and I think she looked at me with the same pissed-off look she'd glared at Tschick with. But I didn't notice.

I said, "Here."

I said, "Beyoncé."

I said, "A drawing."

I said, "For you."

Tatiana stared at the drawing, and before she had looked up from it I heard Tschick say to André, "Nah, no time. We have something to take care of." He nudged me and went back to the car. I followed. Then the engine fired up. I pounded my fist on the dashboard as Tschick shifted into second gear and crept toward the end of the cul-de-sac.

"Want to see something cool?" he asked.

I didn't answer. I couldn't.

"Want to see something cool?" Tschick asked again.

"Do whatever you want!" I yelled. It felt as if a weight had been lifted from my shoulders, such a feeling of relief.

Tschick revved the engine and raced toward the end of the cul-de-sac. Then he yanked the steering wheel first to the right and then the left and pulled the emergency brake at the same time. The car did a 180 right in the middle of the street and I nearly flew out the window.

"That doesn't always work," Tschick said proudly. "Doesn't always work."

He accelerated past the redbrick house and I saw out of the corner of my eye the people on the sidewalk. Time seemed to be standing still. Tatiana stood there with the drawing in her hand, André with his mountain bike, and Natalie had just run around from the side of the house.

The Lada sped into the curve in the road and I pounded on the dashboard.

"Step on it!" I shouted.

"I am."

"Faster!" I yelled, watching my fists pound the dash. Relief does not begin to express the way I felt.

I walked down the dark, narrow corridor. I could hardly make
out a thing. Then I went left into the tunnel where the rails
ran and pressed my back to the wall. I could see the two barrels and an open door. I saw Tschick looking around a corner.
I was right on his heels now and even from behind I could tell
that he had no idea what he was doing. But he kept walking
around like an idiot for another couple minutes, never realiz-
ing I was there. Then he stopped right out in the open. I raised
my shotgun and blasted him in the back. A fountain of blood
sprayed out of him. He dropped to the ground and didn't
move. "Shit," he said, "where do you keep coming from? I
never see you." I switched to the chain gun, obliterated his
corpse, and hopped around.

"Okay, okay, that'll do. You don't have to rub it in, man."
Tschick pressed START AGAIN, but it was hopeless. He just
couldn't figure out the lay of the land. You could follow him
for hours and he never noticed. And I just destroyed him every
time. I was like a world champion at *Doom*, and he didn't have
a clue.

He went and got himself another beer.

"What if we just took off?" he asked.

"What?"

"Go on vacation. We don't have anything else to do. We could just go on vacation like normal people."

"What are you talking about?"

"Hop in the Lada and go."

"That's not exactly how *normal* people do it."

"But we could."

"Nah. Push START."

"Why not?"

"Nah."

"If I kill you," said Tschick. "Let's say, if I kill you once in the next five games. Or, no, make it ten."

"You couldn't kill me if I gave you a hundred chances."

"Ten."

He was concentrating hard. I shoved a handful of chips in my mouth and waited until he had picked up a chain saw. Then I let him chop me to bits.

"Seriously," I said. "Suppose we did."

We'd pissed away almost the entire day. We'd gone swimming twice. Tschick had told me about his brother. And then he'd discovered the beer in the fridge and helped himself to three bottles. I tried to drink one too. I've tasted beer lots of times, but I never like it. It didn't taste any better this time. I managed to choke down three quarters of the bottle anyway, but it didn't have any effect on me.

"What if they tell on us?"

"They're not going to tell on us. If they were going to, they would have done it by now and the police would have been here already. They have no idea that the Lada was stolen. They only saw us for ten seconds. They probably just thought it belonged to my brother or whatever."

"Where do you want to go, anyway?"

"I don't care."

"You know, if you go somewhere, it's helpful to know where you're going."

"We could go visit my relatives. I have a grandfather in Wallachia."

"Where does he actually live?"

"What do you mean? In Wallachia."

"Does he live near here?"

"What?"

"Or somewhere far away, in the middle of nowhere?"

"Not somewhere, man. In Wallachia."

"It's the same thing."

"What's the same thing?"

"The middle of nowhere and Wallachia is the same thing."

"I don't understand."

"Wallachia is just a word, man," I said, polishing off my beer. "It's just an expression! Like East Bumfuck or the sticks."

"It's where my family is from."

"I thought you were from Russia?"

"Yeah, but part of my family is from Wallachia. My grandfather. And my great-aunt and great-grandfather and ... what's so funny?"

"It's like having a grandfather in Hickville or BFE."

"And what's the joke?"

"There's no such place as Hickville! BFE means Bumfuck, Egypt. And Wallachia doesn't exist either. When you say somebody lives in Wallachia it means they live in the boondocks."

"And the boondocks don't exist either?"

"Nope."

"But my grandfather lives there."

"In the boondocks?"

"You're getting on my nerves. My grandfather lives in some dipshit town in a place called Wallachia. And we're going to drive there tomorrow."

He'd gotten serious again, and so had I. "I know a hundred and fifty countries in the world and the names of all their capital cities," I said, grabbing Tschick's beer and taking a swig. "There's no such place as Wallachia."

"My grandfather's cool. He always has a cigarette tucked behind each ear. And only one tooth. I was there when I was five or something."

"What are you, anyway? Russian? Or Wallachian or something?"

"German. I have a passport."

"Yeah, but where are you from?"

"A city called Rostov. It's in Russia. But my family is from all over — Volga Germans, ethnic Germans. Danube Swabians, Wallachians, Jewish Gypsies . . ."

"What?"

"What what?"

"Jewish Gypsies?"

"Yeah, man. And Swabian and Wallachian . . ."

"No such thing."

"As what?"

"Jewish Gypsies. You're talking shit. You're talking nothing but shit."

"Not at all."

"A Jewish Gypsy would be like an English French. There's no such thing."

"Of course there's no such thing as English French," Tschick said. "But there are French Jews. And there are Gypsy Jews."

"Gypsy Jews."

"Exactly. They wear a funny thing on their head and drive around Russia selling carpets. You know what I'm talking about — the things on their heads. Coverings. Coverings on their heads."

"Coverings on their asses, more like. I don't believe a word you are saying."

"You know that movie with what's-his-name?" Tschick really wanted to prove it to me.

"Movies are not real life," I said dismissively. "In real life you can only be one or the other — a Jew or a Gypsy."

"Gypsy isn't a religion, man. Jewish is a religion. A Gypsy is just someone without a home."

"People without homes are Berbers."

"Berbers are carpets," said Tschick.

I thought about it for a while longer, and when I asked Tschick one last time whether he was *really* Jewish Gypsy and he nodded solemnly, I believed him.

What I still didn't believe was the crap about his grandfather. Because I knew for a fact that Wallachia was just a made-up word. I tried a hundred different ways to prove to Tschick that there was no such place as Wallachia. But I noticed the only time my words made any impact at all was when I made a couple of grand arm gestures as I talked. Tschick mimicked the gestures. Then he went to get more beer. He asked whether I wanted another one too. But I just wanted a Coke.

I was really wound up. And as I watched a fly flitting around the table, I had the feeling that the fly was wound up too — because I was. I'd never had such a good time before. Tschick put two bottles of beer down on the table and said, "You'll see. My grandfather and my great-aunt and my six cousins — four of them are girls, and they're as pretty as orchids. You'll see."

My mind was soon occupied with thoughts of the cousins. But Tschick had no sooner left the house than the images of his cousins and everything disappeared into the ether, leaving only a feeling of misery. It had nothing to do with Tschick. It had to do with Tatiana. It had to do with the fact that I had no idea what she thought of me now, and that I might never find out. And at that moment I would have given anything to be in Wallachia or anywhere else in the world but Berlin.

Before I went to bed, I opened my laptop. I had four e-mails from my father complaining that I'd switched off my cell phone and wasn't answering the landline. I had to think up some excuse and would need to write him an e-mail back saying that everything was going great here. Which it was. And since I didn't feel like writing the e-mail and couldn't think of a good excuse, I looked up Wallachia on Wikipedia. That's when my mind *really* started to race.

Early Sunday morning. Four o'clock. Tschick had said that would be the best time. Four A.M., dead of night. I had barely slept at all, just dozed on and off a little, and I was instantly wide awake when I heard footsteps on our terrace. I ran to the door and there was Tschick, standing in the darkness with a duffel bag. We whispered even though there was no reason to whisper. Tschick threw his duffel down in the hall and we set off to retrieve the car.

When we'd driven back from Werder, he'd parked the Lada where it was normally parked, which was about a ten-minute walk from my house. A fox crossed the sidewalk right in front of us, heading in the direction of downtown. A garbage truck whooshed by us and we passed a coughing old lady walking in the opposite direction. We actually stood out more in the middle of the night than we would have during the day. About thirty meters from the car, Tschick gave me the signal to wait. I stood in some bushes and felt my heart racing. Tschick pulled a yellow tennis ball out of his duffel bag. He pressed it on the door handle of the Lada and hit it with the flat of his hand. I couldn't imagine what good it would do, but Tschick rasped, "Professional on the job!"

The door opened. He waved me over.

Inside he fiddled with the wires and the engine fired up. He hit the bumpers of both the car in front of us and the one behind us as he tried to get out of the parking spot. I huddled down in the passenger seat and examined the tennis ball. It was a normal tennis ball with a finger-sized hole cut into it.

"Does that work on all kinds of cars?"

"No, not all of them. But ones with central locking — it creates a vacuum." He scraped his way out of the parking spot as I pressed and squeezed the tennis ball in my hand. I just couldn't see how it worked. Russians!

Ten minutes later we were loading up the Lada. There's a door directly from our house to our garage, so we carried everything we thought we needed out that way. First off was bread — along with crackers and various spreads and a couple jars of jam. We figured we'd want to eat at some point. And to do that we also needed plates and knives and spoons. We threw in a three-man tent, sleeping bags, and sleeping mats. Then we took out the mats and replaced them with air mattresses. Half the household ended up in the car after a while, and then we started taking stuff back out again. Most of it you don't really need. There was a lot of back and forth. We fought about whether we'd need Rollerblades, for instance. Tschick said that if we ran out of gas, one of us could Rollerblade to a gas station. But I figured we might as well just throw in the fold-able bicycle for that. Or just go by bike instead of car. We were nearly done when we decided to bring a case of bottled water, and that turned out to be the best idea of all. Or rather the only good idea at all. Because everything else proved useless: bad-minton racquets, a huge stack of manga, four pairs of shoes, my dad's toolbox, six frozen pizzas. One thing we didn't take were cell phones. "So the cocksuckers can't tell where we are," said Tschick.

And also no CDs. The Lada had big speakers in the back but only an old lint-stuffed cassette player bolted under the glove box. But to be honest I was just as happy not to have to listen to Beyoncé in the car. And of course we took the two hundred Euros as well as what money I had of my own. I wasn't sure what we would use it for. In my mind we'd be driving through unpopulated wastelands — practically deserts. I hadn't studied Wikipedia enough to have seen what it looked like down closer to Wallachia. But I definitely couldn't imagine there was much going on there.

I had hung my arm out the window and put my head down on it. We were driving at a leisurely pace through pastures and fields as the sun slowly rose somewhere beyond Rahnsdorf. It was the weirdest and most beautiful thing I'd ever experienced. I can't pinpoint what was so weird about it, because it was just a car ride, and that was nothing new. But there's a difference between sitting in a car with adults who are talking about construction-grade concrete and Angela Merkel, and being in a car with no adults and no chitchat. Tschick had hung his arm out the window too and was guiding the Lada up a little hill with his right hand. It was as if the thing was driving itself through the fields. It was a totally different sort of car ride, a totally different world. Everything seemed bigger, the colors brighter, the noises as if they were in surround sound. It wouldn't have surprised me a bit if all of a sudden Tony Soprano or a dinosaur or a spaceship had appeared on the road in front of us.

We took the most direct route out of Berlin, leaving the early-morning bustle behind us, and then wound our way through the villages on the outskirts of town on back roads and quiet country lanes. Which is where we realized we hadn't brought a map. All we had was a map of Berlin.

"Maps are for pussies," said Tschick. And he was right, of course. But there was an obvious problem with that logic: How would we ever find our way to Wallachia when we couldn't even find Rahnsdorf? So we decided just to head south. Wallachia was in Romania, and Romania was south.

The next problem was that we didn't know which way was south. There were already storm clouds in the sky that morning, and you couldn't see the sun. It was sweltering outside; much hotter and more humid than the day before.

I had a little compass on my keychain — got it out of a gumball machine one time. It didn't seem to point south inside the car and when I tried it outside the needle spun all over the place. We stopped just to try it out, and when I got back in the car I noticed there was something under the mat in the footwell. It was a cassette — *The Solid Gold Collection*, by Richard Clayderman. But it wasn't real music. It was just some tinkling on the piano, Mozart or something. We didn't have anything else to play, and we thought maybe something else had been taped over it, so we listened to it all the way through. Forty-five minutes. The idiot. Though I have to admit that even after Richard and his piano had made us puke, we flipped it over and listened to the other side, which had exactly the same kind of crap on it. Better than nothing. Seriously, though, I didn't tell Tschick at the time and I'm not proud saying it now, but the minor-key stuff really took the wind out of my sails. I kept thinking about Tatiana and the way she had looked at me when I gave her the drawing. And then we were rattling down the autobahn to "Ballade pour Adeline."

Somehow we'd strayed onto a road that dumped us onto the autobahn. Tschick could drive okay, but he had never experienced anything like a German autobahn. Dealing with it took all he had. When he was supposed to merge, he stepped on the brakes, hit the gas, braked again, and then weaved along the shoulder at a snail's pace before he finally managed to swerve left into the lane. Luckily nobody rammed us from behind. I was pressing my feet against the floorboard with every ounce of my strength. And I thought if we died, Richard and his piano would be to blame. But we didn't die. The rattling in the Lada kept getting louder and louder and we decided we'd get off at the next exit and stick to little local roads. There was another problem with the autobahn too: A man in a black Mercedes pulled up alongside and looked across at us, making wild gestures. He was flashing numbers with his fingers and held up his cell phone and seemed to be trying to write down our license plate number. I was scared shitless, but Tschick just nodded as if to thank the guy for telling us we still had our lights on. Then we lost him in traffic.

Tschick did look older than fourteen. But no way did he look eighteen — old enough to drive. Though we had no idea what he looked like at full speed through the filthy windows of the Lada. We decided to do a few experiments on a dirt road after we'd gotten off the autobahn to see how he could best come across as an adult. I stood on the side of the road and Tschick drove past me about twenty times. He started by sitting on top of our sleeping bags and putting my sunglasses on top of his head. He tried smoking a cigarette. He ripped some pieces of duct tape and stuck them on his face to simulate a goatee. But he just looked like a fourteen-year-old with duct tape on his face. Then he took the tape off except for a little strip under his nose. He looked like Hitler that way, but from afar it actually made him look older. And since we were now out in the politically backward state of Brandenburg, nobody would take offense.

So the only thing we still had to deal with was our lack of orientation. But we saw a sign to Dresden, and Dresden was definitely south of Berlin. So we went that way. Whenever we had a choice of roads we took the smaller, less trafficked option. And along those roads the signs only indicated the next tiny town rather than Dresden. How did you know whether Burig or Freienbrink was farther south? We flipped coins. Tschick loved flipping coins to decide. He said we should make all our decisions on the route that way. Heads we turned right, tails left, and if it stayed upright on its edge we would go straight. But obviously it never stayed upright so we never made any forward progress. So we quickly abandoned the coin flip and just went right-left, right-left. That was my suggestion, but it was no better. In theory, if you keep turning right and then left, you'll never drive in a circle. But we managed to drive in a circle. When we passed a sign for the third time that said Markgrafpieske to the left and Spreenhagen to the right, Tschick came up with the idea of only going toward places that began with the letter *M* or *T*. But there were too few of them. I suggested looking at how far away places were according to what was listed on the signs and heading to ones where the distance was a prime number. But at a sign that said BAD FREIEN-WALDE 51 KILOMETERS we mistakenly turned that way and by the time we realized it was three times seventeen we were already at another crossing.

Eventually the sun came through the clouds. The road forked in the middle of a cornfield. To the left the road was cobblestone. To the right, dirt. We fought over which way was south. The sun wasn't quite in the middle. It was a few minutes before eleven o'clock in the morning.

"That's south," said Tschick.

"No, that's east."

We got out and ate a couple chocolate-coated cookies that were already partly melted. The bugs in the cornfield were making an overwhelming buzz.

"You know an ordinary watch can show you the points of a compass?" Tschick took off his watch. It was an old Russian model, the kind you have to wind. He held it out between us, but I didn't know how the trick worked, and he didn't either. I think you're supposed to aim one hand at the sun, and then the other one will point north. Something like that. But if we aimed one hand at the sun at eleven in the morning, both hands pointed in the same direction — and that was definitely not north.

"Maybe it points south?" said Tschick.

"What — and half an hour from now south is that way?"

"Or maybe it's because of daylight savings? It doesn't work in summer. I'll turn it back an hour."

"What will that change? The hands turn completely around in the space of an hour, but north and south aren't constantly shifting around."

"Yeah, but if a compass spins — maybe it's a gyrocompass."

"A gyrocompass?"

"You've never heard of a gyrocompass?"

"A gyrocompass has nothing to do with a gyroscope. It doesn't spin," I said. "It works with alcohol — there's alcohol inside it."

"You're pulling my leg."

"I know that from a book about a ship that capsizes. One of the sailors is an alcoholic, and he breaks open the gyrocompass to drink the fluid inside. And they have no way to orient themselves."

"Doesn't sound like a true story."

"It's true. The book is called *The Sea-Bear* or *The Sea-Wolf*, I think."

"You mean Steppenwolf. That's also about drugs. That's the kind of stuff my brother reads."

"Steppenwolf is a *band*," I say.

"Well, I'd say if we don't know which way is south, we should just take the dirt road," said Tschick, strapping his watch back on his wrist. "Less likely to see other cars."

As always, he was right. It was a good decision. We didn't come across another car for an hour. We were someplace where there weren't even any houses on the horizon. In one field there were pumpkins as big as medicine balls.

The wind picked up, and the wind died down again. The sun disappeared behind dark clouds, and two raindrops fell on the windshield. The drops were so big that they wet almost the entire windshield. Tschick drove faster as tall trees bent in the wind. Suddenly a gust of wind blew our car practically across the street. Tschick turned into a bumpy track that cut between two fields of wheat. The tinkling piano seemed more dramatic now. And then, after one kilometer, the farm road just stopped, right in the middle of the field.

"I'm not driving back now," said Tschick, rumbling forward without even braking. The stalks of wheat crackled against the fenders and doors. Tschick let the vehicle coast in the field, downshifted, and stepped on the gas. The engine revved and the grille of the Lada parted the sea of golden wheat like a snowplow. Though the Lada was making strange noises, it plowed through the field effortlessly. But it was tough to tell which way we were going. You couldn't see over the stalks of wheat. No horizon to aim for. Another drop of rain fell on the windshield. The field started to slope gently upward. We must have meandered and turned because we came across a section of grain we'd already plowed a path through. I told

Tschick we should try to write our names in the field — somebody in a helicopter could read them. Or maybe we could see our names on Google Earth. But we lost our sense of direction when we were crossing the first T. We just drove around, then went up a hill again and when we got to the top the wheat suddenly ended. Tschick braked at the last second. The back of the car was still in the grain. The front of the Lada peeked out at the landscape. A lush green cow pasture sloped steeply away below us, giving us a wide-open view over endless fields, groups of trees, farm roads, hills and ridges, mountains, meadows, and woods. Clouds were lined up on the horizon and you could see lightning hitting the steeple of a distant church, but you couldn't hear any thunder. It was dead quiet. The fourth raindrop plopped down on the windshield. Tschick turned off the engine. I turned off the cassette player.

We just sat there looking out over the landscape for a few minutes. Smaller white clouds floated along below the dark storm clouds. Blue-gray mist swirled around the distant ridges and some ridges closer by. The dark clouds swelled and billowed toward us.

"Independence Day," said Tschick.

We pulled out bread and jam and a couple of Cokes, and as we were setting up for a picnic in the car, it got very dark. It was early afternoon, but it was suddenly as dark as night outside. Just then I saw a cow fall over in one of the meadows. At first I thought I was seeing things, but Tschick saw it too. All the other cattle had turned their butts into the wind, but the one just fell over. Then the wind stopped as quickly as it had started. For a moment, nothing happened. It was so dark you couldn't read the labels on the soda bottles. Then it sounded like a bucket of water had splashed onto our windshield and the rain hit us like a wall.

It lasted for hours. It crashed and thundered and poured. A tree bough as thick as my arm and covered with foliage went flying across the valley below us as if some kid was flying it like a kite. When it finally stopped raining that evening, the entire wheat field behind us had been matted down, and the pasture in front of us had been turned into a swamp. It would have been impossible to drive in any direction. We were stuck. So we spent our first night sleeping in the car on top of that hill. It wasn't terribly comfortable, but given the mud all around us, there wasn't any alternative.

I didn't sleep much, but luckily that meant that at first light I saw the farmer driving his tractor through the valley below us. I didn't know whether he'd seen us, but I woke up Tschick and he immediately started the car. We inched backward through the wheat, more coasting than driving down the hill, and at some point hit the road again. Off we went.

The chocolate cookies were edible again, and after we ate them for breakfast, Tschick tried to teach me how to drive in a meadow next to some woods. I wasn't crazy about the idea at first, but Tschick said it was embarrassing to steal cars when you couldn't even drive. He also accused me of being scared, which I was.

Tschick did a practice run so I could watch exactly what he was doing — which pedals he was pushing and how he shifted. I'd seen my parents drive a million times, but I never really paid attention to how they did things. I didn't even know which pedal was which.

"The clutch is on the left. You let that up very slowly and step on the gas pedal at the same time — see? See?"

Of course I didn't see a thing. Let the pedal up? Step on the gas? Tschick showed me.

When you start, you put it in first gear. But you have to stand on the clutch and also, with your right foot, tap the gas pedal. Then you have to let up the clutch and give it gas at the same time. That's the most difficult part — getting the car going when it's standing still. It took me twenty tries before I got the Lada rolling, and then when I finally did I was so surprised that I pulled up both my feet — and the car jumped and then the engine cut out.

"Just step on the clutch and you won't stall. The same thing when you brake — push the clutch at the same time or else the engine will stall."

It took a while before I could brake properly. You're supposed to push the brake pedal with your right foot, but I couldn't get that through my head at first. For whatever reason, I kept stepping on it with both feet. Once I'd finally mastered everything and got the car rolling, I cruised around the meadow in first gear and it was amazing. The Lada actually did what I wanted it to do. When I got going a little faster, the engine really started to whine and Tschick told me to step on the clutch for three full seconds. I stood on the pedal and Tschick shifted into second gear for me.

"Now step on the gas!" he said, and suddenly I shot off. Fortunately the meadow was huge. I practiced for a few hours. That's how long it took before I could get the car going and shift up to third gear and back down again without constantly stalling. I was drenched with sweat, but I didn't want to stop. Tschick was sunning himself on the air mattress at the edge of the woods. The only people we saw all day were two walkers who passed by without even noticing us. At some point I skidded to a stop next to Tschick and asked how he hotwired the car. Now that I could drive, I wanted to know about everything else too.

Tschick pushed his sunglasses onto the top of his head, hopped into the driver's seat, and rummaged around in the mess of wires beneath the steering wheel. "You have to connect this wire, the steady-plus wire, number thirty, which is connected to the battery, to the one that runs power to the car's electrical system when the key is turned — number fifteen. See, thirty to fifteen. The duct tape is holding them together. You have to wrap it around there real thick. Once they are connected, the ignition system has power. Then you just touch the starter relay wire — this one, the number fifty — to those two wires. Done."

"And that works for any car?"

"I've only ever tried it on this one. But my brother says it'll work on any car. Fifteen, thirty, and fifty."

"And that's it?"

"The only other thing you have to do is break the locking pin on the steering column. The rest is easy-peasy. To free up the steering wheel, you put your foot here, and boom, done. And obviously you have to bypass the fuel pump."

Obviously. Bypass the fuel pump. I didn't say anything for a minute. We'd learned about electrical currents in physics class. That there was plus and minus, and that the electrons flowed through wires like water and all that. But that seemed to have nothing to do with what was happening in our Lada. Steady-plus? It sounded as if a completely different sort of electricity was flowing in this car than in the wires in physics class. Like we'd landed in some alternate reality. But maybe physics class was the alternate reality. Because the fact that Tschick's system worked showed he must be right.

Tschick drove back onto the road. After we'd passed a bakery in a little village, we both got the itch for a coffee. We parked the car in some bushes outside town and walked back to the bakery. There we bought coffee and fresh rolls topped with cheese and cold cuts. And just as I was about to bite into my roll, somebody behind me said, "Klingenberg, what are you doing here?"

Lutz Heckel, the tub of lard on stilts, was sitting at a table behind us. Sitting next to him was an even bigger tub of lard on stilts and a not quite as big tub of lard on more solid columns.

"And the Mongolian's here too," Heckel said, surprised, but also in a tone that left no doubt as to what he felt about Mongols in general and about Tschick in particular.

"Visiting relatives," I said and turned quickly away. It didn't seem like a good time for an extended conversation.

"I didn't know you had relatives around here."

"I do," said Tschick, raising his cup of coffee like he was making a toast. "There's a detention center in Zwietow."

I couldn't remember seeing Heckel at Tatiana's party, but

the next thing he asked us was *how* we'd gotten here. Tschick made up something about a bicycle tour.

"Schoolmates of yours?" I heard the big tub of lard ask, and then I didn't hear much of anything for a while. At some point I heard car keys rattle on the table behind us and the chairs were pushed back. Daddy Heckel walked past us on his stilts and went back up to the counter. He came back with an armload of rolls, put four of them down on our table, and said, "Gotta make sure our bikers have enough energy out there on the road!" Then he rapped his knuckles on the table as a good-bye, and the tub of lard family walked off across the town square.

"Uh," Tschick said.

I didn't know what to say either.

We sat in front of the bakery for a good long time. We'd really needed the coffee. And the bread.

Every half an hour a bus packed with tourists rolled into the town square. There was a little castle somewhere in town. Tschick was sitting with his back to the square, where the buses stopped and let people off, but I had to look at the senior citizens spilling out of the buses. Because the tourists were all old. They were all wearing brown or beige clothing and stupid-looking hats, and when they passed the spot where we were sitting — which was slightly uphill from where the buses stopped — they were huffing and puffing like they'd just finished running a marathon.

I could never imagine becoming so old, being all beige like that. All the old men I knew looked like that. And the old women. They were beige. It was incredibly difficult to conceive of the fact that these old women must have once been young. That they had once been the same age as Tatiana, and that they had gotten dressed up and gone out to dance at places where people referred to them as "hot dishes" or whatever they said fifty or a hundred years ago. Not all of them, of course. Some of them were dull or ugly even then, no doubt. But even the dull and ugly ones probably had dreams about how their lives would pan out. They must have had plans for the future. Even the totally normal ones had plans for the future. And what I guarantee was not in those plans was becoming a beige senior citizen. The more I thought about these old folks who kept climbing out of the buses, the more depressed I got. The thing that got to me the most was the thought that even among the people on these bus tours, there must have been some who weren't boring or dull when they were young. Some had been attractive. Some were the prettiest girls in their class even — the ones everybody had a crush on. And seventy years ago some kid probably sat in a playground fort and got excited when he saw the light go on in some of these old ladies' rooms. But those girls had become beige senior citizens too, and you couldn't tell them apart from the rest. They all had gray skin and fleshy noses and ears now, and it made me so depressed that I practically threw up.

"Psst," said Tschick, looking past me. I followed his gaze and spotted two policemen walking along a row of parked cars looking at every license plate number. Without a word, we took our paper cups and sauntered casually back to the bushes where we had parked the Lada. Then we drove back the way we had come that morning, back along a country road, out of there like a shot. We didn't have to talk long about what we would do next.

In a wooded area not far away, we found a parking lot where people parked to go hiking. We started looking for a license plate we could unscrew, but it wasn't easy to find one. Most of the plates weren't even attached with screws. Fortunately there were quite a few cars there. And finally we found an old VW Beetle with Munich plates. We attached our plates to the VW in the hopes that the owner wouldn't immediately notice his were gone.

Then we drove a few miles on dirt paths that crisscrossed fields before taking a little road into a forest and then pulling over at an abandoned sawmill. We stuffed our backpacks and hiked off into the woods.

We weren't planning to ditch the Lada, but despite switching the license plates we weren't too confident about the whole situation. It seemed like the smartest thing to do was to keep it off the road for a while. We could spend a day or two in the woods. That was the plan. Though we didn't have a real plan. We didn't really know if they were looking for us or not. And whether they would give up after a few days if they were looking for us.

We hiked up a trail, and as we rose higher on the ridge the woods thinned out a bit. Eventually we came to an observation platform with a cool view out over the area. But even better than the view was the fact that there was a snack stand there selling water and candy and ice cream. So we wouldn't starve. And we decided to stay near the snack stand. Not far below the scenic lookout was a steep meadow. We found a quiet spot there below a giant elderberry bush. We lay down in the sun and snoozed the day away. Late in the day we loaded ourselves up with Snickers and Cokes and crawled into our sleeping bags and listened to the crickets start to chirp. During the day, hikers, bikers, and buses had come and gone constantly to the observation platform, but when it started to get dark we had the entire mountain to ourselves. It was still warm, almost too warm, and Tschick, who had managed to get the owner of the snack stand to sell him two beers at the end of the day, popped them open with a lighter.

More and more stars appeared in the sky above us. We lay on our backs and watched as the spaces between the stars filled with smaller stars, and then even tinier stars came into view between the smaller stars. The blackness kept retreating.

"It's amazing," said Tschick.

"Yeah," I said. "It is amazing."

"It's way better than TV. Though TV's good too. You ever seen *Star Wars*?"

"Of course."

"You seen *Starship Troopers*?"

"Is that the one with the monkeys?"

"No, bugs."

"And a brain bug at the end? A giant brain with — with slimy things sticking out of it?"

"Yeah!"

"That's an amazing movie."

"Yeah, it is amazing."

"Can you imagine? Somewhere up there, on some star — that's what's happening! Actual bugs are taking over some planet, slaughtering all the inhabitants, and nobody even knows about it," I said. "Except for us."

"Right, except for us."

"But we're the only ones who realize it. And the bugs don't know that we know."

"Seriously? Do you really think so?" Tschick rose to his elbows and looked at me. "Do you think there really is something out there? I mean, not necessarily bugs. But something?"

"I don't know. I heard one time that you can calculate the probability of there being other life in the universe. The chances are very slim, but since the universe is infinitely large, if you multiply even the slimmest odds by infinity you get a number — a number of planets where there's probably life. It worked here, after all. So somewhere out there I guarantee there are giant bugs."

"That's exactly what I think, exactly what I think!" Tschick lay back down on his back and looked intensely at the sky. "Amazing, isn't it?"

"Yeah, amazing."

"It just blows me away."

"And just imagine: The bugs go to the bug movies! They make movies on their planet and they're sitting in some bug cinema watching a movie set on Earth — it's about two kids who steal a car."

"And it's a horror film!" says Tschick. "The bugs think we're disgusting because we're *not* slimy."

"But they all think it's just science fiction, and that we don't exist in reality. People and cars — what a load of crap! Nobody watching the movie thinks it could be true."

"Except for two young bugs! They think it could be real. Two young school bugs who have just stolen an army helicopter. They're flying around the bug planet thinking the same thing we are. They think we exist because we think they exist."

"Crazy!"

"Yeah, crazy."

I looked up at the stars extending out into incomprehensible infinity and was somehow frightened. I was moved and frightened at the same time. I thought about the bugs. I could almost see them up there in some flickering little galaxy. Then I turned to Tschick and he looked at me, looked me right in the eyes, and said that everything was amazing. And it was. It was truly amazing.

And the crickets chirped the entire night.

When I woke up in the morning, I was alone. I looked around. There was a light fog clinging to the meadow and no sign of Tschick. But since his air mattress was still there I didn't think much of it. I tried to go back to sleep, but at some point my uneasiness got the better of me. I went up to the observation platform and looked in every direction. I was the only person on the mountain. The snack stand wasn't open yet. The sun looked like a red peach in a bowl of milk, and with the first beams of sunshine came a group of cyclists riding up the road. Not even ten minutes later, Tschick came tromping up the hill too. He had walked down to the sawmill to check on the Lada and see if it was still there. It was still there. We went back and forth for a while on what to do, and then decided that we would go back down now and drive on after all. Waiting around made no sense.

While we were talking, the group of bicyclists had spread out and sat down on a low wall near the observation deck — a dozen kids our age and one adult. They were eating breakfast and talking quietly among themselves, and there was something really weird about them. The group was too small to be a school class or summer camp, too big to be a family, and too well dressed to be from a loony bin or orphanage. Something was off about them. Their clothes were strange. They weren't brand-name clothes, but they didn't look cheap either. On the contrary. They looked expensive — but uncool. And they all had really clean faces. I don't really know how to describe it, but their faces were somehow cleaner than normal. The weirdest one of all was the chaperone. He talked to them like he was their boss. Tschick asked one of the girls what institution they'd escaped from and she said, "We're not from an institution. We're Mobile Nobles. We're riding from manor house to manor house." She said it very seriously and very politely. Maybe she was putting us on and this was a bike tour organized by the local clown school.

"And you guys?" she said.

"What about us?"

"Are you also on a bicycle tour?"

"We're motorists," Tschick said.

The girl turned to the boy next to her and said, "You were wrong. They are motorists."

"And you guys are what exactly? Mobile Nobles?"

"What's so strange about that? Is *motorist* somehow less weird?"

"Yes, but *mobile nobles*?"

"And you guys are the proletariat in a chariot?"

Man, they were mean. Maybe the stash of cocaine had gone missing at the local clown school. We never figured out what those kids were really doing up there on the mountain, though we did come across them a little while later on the road. We passed them in the Lada and the girls waved and we waved back. Don't know about the nobility, but at least the mobility was true. For some reason we felt unbelievably confident again from that point on. And Tschick also suggested that if we needed to use code names, he would be Count Tschickula and I would be Count Lada.

CHAPTER TWENTY-FIVE

The problem we had that morning, however, was that we had nothing to eat.

We'd brought some cans of stuff but no can opener. There were a couple crackers but nothing to put on them. And the six frozen pizzas were thawed and absolutely inedible. I tried to use a lighter to grill a piece of one of them, but it didn't work. In the end, six Frisbees flew out of the Lada like UFOs fleeing the burning death star.

Relief came a few kilometers down the road. A sign pointed left to a little village, and on the same signpost was an ad for a supermarket one kilometer away. We took the left and you could see the huge store from a long way off, sitting there like a shoe box plopped down in the landscape.

The adjacent village was tiny. We drove through and parked by a big barn, where nobody would see us, and then walked back into town. Even though the entire village consisted of maybe ten streets that all met at a fountain in the town square, we couldn't figure out which direction we needed to go to get to the supermarket. Tschick thought we needed to go left. I thought we should go straight. And there was nobody on the street to ask. We wandered through totally empty village streets until finally a boy on a bike appeared. It was a wooden balance bike with no pedals. He had to move his legs like he was running in order to push the thing along. He was probably twelve, meaning he was about ten years too old for the bike. His knees dragged on the ground. He stopped right in front of us and gaped at us with huge eyes — like a mutated frog or something.

Tschick asked him where the supermarket was and the kid smiled — a smile that said that he was either confident or clueless. He had huge gums.

"We don't shop at the supermarket," he said decisively.

"Interesting. But where is it?"

"We shop at Froehlich's market."

"Aha, at Froehlich's." Tschick nodded at the kid like a cowboy who didn't want to have to hurt another cowboy. "What we're really interested in is how to get to the supermarket."

The boy nodded eagerly, lifted a hand to his head as if he was going to scratch himself, and then motioned indistinctly with the other hand. Finally he stuck out his pointer finger and aimed it between two houses. There, on the horizon, was a farmstead set among tall poplar trees. "There's Froehlich's! That's where we always shop."

"Fantastic," said Tschick. "And now, one more time, where is the supermarket?"

His gums made it clear that we probably weren't going to get an answer. But there was nobody else on the street we could ask.

"What do you guys want to do there?"

"What do we want to do there? Mike, Mikey — what do we want to do at the supermarket again?"

"Do you want to get stuff or just have a look around?" asked the boy.

"Look around? Do you go to the supermarket to look around?"

"Come on, let's go," I said. "We'll find it." And to the boy, "We want to buy some food."

There was no point in making fun of the boy with the frog eyes.

Just then a tall, very pale woman stepped out of a house and called, "Friedemann! Come inside, Friedemann, it's noon!"

"I'm coming," answered the boy, and his voice had changed. He had taken on the same singsong tone as his mother.

"Why do you want to buy food?" he asked. Tschick had already walked over to the woman to ask the way to the supermarket.

"To the what?"

"The supermarket," said Friedemann.

"Oh, the big store," said the woman. She had a strange-looking face. Emaciated but not unhealthy looking. She said, "We don't shop there. We shop at Froehlich's."

"So we've heard." Tschick put on his most polite smile. He was good at it. Though I had the feeling he overdid it a little sometimes. Still, the fact that he looked like a Mongolian invader balanced things back out.

"Why would you want to go there?"

Oh, Christ, was the entire family like this? Didn't any of them know what you do at a supermarket?

"Go shopping," I said.

"Shopping," said the woman, drawing her arms to her chest as if to keep herself from accidentally pointing the way to the supermarket.

"Food! They want to buy food," squealed Friedemann.

The woman looked at us suspiciously and then asked if we were from around here and what we wanted here. Tschick told her a story about a bicycle tour, crossing East Germany, and the woman looked up and down the street. Not a bike in sight.

"And we have a flat," I said and, like Friedemann, gestured vaguely in no particular direction. "But we really need to do some shopping because we haven't had breakfast. . . ."

Nothing in her facial expression or her manner changed, but she said, "We have lunch at noon and you are very welcome to join us, you young men from Berlin. You will be our guests."

Then she showed her gums too — not quite as much as Friedemann, but a lot. Friedemann spun his balance bike around and shot toward the house, letting out a sound that was apparently a scream of excitement. There were now three or four smaller children standing at the door to the house all staring at us with big frog eyes.

I didn't know what to say, and Tschick didn't know either.

"What's for lunch?" he finally said. They were having something called Risi Bisi. Whatever that was. I scratched my head and Tschick went for a grand finale. He opened his eyes wide, bowed slightly, and said, "That sounds fantastic, ma'am."

Oh, Christ, I couldn't believe it. That must have been lesson two from the German classes they give to immigrants.

"Why did you do that?" I whispered as we headed inside behind the woman. Tschick waved his arms as if to say, "What else was I supposed to do?"

Before we could follow her into the house she nodded to Friedemann, who took us by the hands and led us around the side of the house into the backyard. I didn't like the situation. It also made me uneasy that, when Friedemann looked away for a second, Tschick made a sign with his finger that Friedemann was crazy.

In the backyard was a big white wooden table with ten chairs around it. Four of them were already taken by Friedemann's siblings. The oldest one was a girl who was maybe nine, and the youngest was a boy of about six. And all of them looked alike. The mother brought out the food in a huge pot. Apparently this was Risi Bisi: rice in a yellowish goop, with little chunks and green herbs floating in it. The mother served everyone a bowl with a soup ladle, but nobody touched their food. Instead, they all lifted their arms as if on command and joined hands. And since the entire family was looking at us now, we also lifted our hands. I linked hands with Tschick and Friedemann, and the mother lowered her head and said, "Okay, maybe we don't necessarily have to do this today. We welcome our guests, who have traveled from far away, to the day's festivities and give thanks for everything that is bestowed upon us. *Guten Appetit*."

Then everyone shook hands and we ate. Say what you will, but the goopy rice tasted fantastic.

When we were finished, Tschick pushed his empty bowl away with both hands and, in the woman's direction, said that it had been a scrumtrulescent meal. The woman reacted by furrowing her brow. I scratched my head and added that it had been ages since I had eaten so well. Then Tschick said it had been super scrumtrulescent. The woman showed a little of her gums and cleared her throat in her fist, and Friedemann looked at us with his big frog eyes. And then came dessert. Holy crap.

I'd rather not even tell the next part. But I will anyway. Florentine, the nine-year-old, brought the dessert out on a tray. It was something foamy and white topped with raspberries. There were eight individual bowls of it. Eight different-sized bowls. I figured there'd be a fight over the biggest bowl. But I was wrong.

The eight bowls sat huddled together in the middle of the table and nobody touched them. Everyone just shifted in their chairs and looked at the woman.

"Quickly, quickly!" said Friedemann.

"First I have to think," she said and closed her eyes for a moment. "Okay, I have it." She cast a friendly look at me and Tschick and then looked around the table again. "What did Merope Gaunt get for Slytherin's locket when she . . ."

"Twelve galleons!" shouted Friedemann, jumping in his seat and shaking the table.

"Ten galleons," said all the others.

The mother pensively rocked from side to side and then smiled. "I believe Elisabeth was first."

Elisabeth coolly grabbed the biggest bowl with the most raspberries. Florentine protested because she thought she'd shouted the answer at the same time, and Friedemann pounded on the table shouting, "Ten! I'm an idiot! Ten!"

Tschick kicked me under the table. I shrugged. Slytherin? Galleons?

"You've never read Harry Potter?" asked the mother. "Oh well, it doesn't matter. We're changing subjects now."

She thought for another moment and while she did, Elisabeth took a little spoonful of her dessert, held it to her lips, and waited. She waited until Friedemann looked at her; then she slowly put the spoon into her mouth.

"Geography and science," said the mother. "What was the name of the research vessel Alexander von Humboldt . . ."

"Pizarro!" cried Friedemann as his chair fell backward. He immediately took the second biggest bowl, put his nose to the rim, and whispered, "Ten, ten. How did I ever come up with twelve?"

"That's not fair," said Florentine. "I knew the answer too. It's just because he yelled."

Next the mother asked what was celebrated on Pentecost. I probably don't have to tell you how the game played out. When the two smallest bowls were left, the mother asked who had been the first president of the Federal Republic of Germany. I said Adenauer and Tschick said Helmut Kohl. The mother wanted to give us our desserts anyway, but Florentine was against that. And so were the rest of the children. I would happily have forfeited my dessert at that point. Jonas, the youngest of all the children, about six years old, rattled off the names of all the presidents of the Federal Republic of Germany, starting with the correct answer, Theodor Heuss, and then took charge of the game himself. He asked us what the capital of Germany was.

"Uh, I would say Berlin," I said.

"That's what I would have said, as well," said Tschick, nodding earnestly.

Say what you will, but the dish once again was fantastic. I swear I've never tasted such delicious foam with raspberries.

Afterward we thanked the family for the excellent meal and were about to leave when Tschick said, "I have a question for you. How do you figure out which way is north with a watch when it's . . ."

"You aim the hour hand at the sun! Then you wind the minute hand to twelve and it is pointing south!" yelled Friedemann.

"Correct," said Tschick, pushing him his bowl with the last few raspberries in it.

"I knew that too," said Florentine. "It's just because he always yells."

"I might have gotten that," said Jonas, sticking his finger in his ear. "But maybe I wouldn't really have known that. I'm not sure. Would I have known that?" He looked quizzically at his mother, and his mother patted his head lovingly and nodded as if to say he would surely have known the answer.

They all walked us to the gate to say good-bye, and they gave us a huge pumpkin to take with us. It was just sitting there, a huge pumpkin, and they said we should take it in case we got hungry. We took it but didn't know what to say. They waved good-bye for a long time as we wandered off.

"Cool people," said Tschick. I wasn't sure whether he was serious or not. I didn't think he could be serious since he'd made the twirling-finger this-kid-is-crazy sign when we'd walked in. But his facial expression made it clear he was serious. I guess he was serious about both things. He was serious that the kid was crazy and that he thought they were "cool people." He was right too: They were cool, crazy people. They were nice and they were nuts, they made great food and knew a lot of stuff — just not the location of the supermarket. That they didn't know.

But we finally found it anyway. Later, as we turned into the street where the Lada was parked, carrying two huge bags of groceries and a giant pumpkin, I put the pumpkin down on the curb and went behind a bush to take a piss. Tschick trudged on without turning around — I'm only describing all of this in such detail because it proved important.

When I came out of the bushes, Tschick was about a hundred meters ahead of me and just a few steps from the Lada. I picked up the pumpkin and at the same moment a man carrying a bicycle came out of a driveway between me and Tschick. He lifted the bike up, flipped it over, and put it down on its seat and handlebars. The man was wearing a yellow shirt, greenish pants, and clip-in shoes. On the bike rack was a white hat that fell off when he turned it upside down. It was only when I looked at the hat on the ground that I recognized it as a policeman's cap. I also noticed something else we hadn't seen when we'd parked on the street: On the little brick house in front of the barn was a sign hanging with the green and white logo of the police. It was the town sheriff's place.

The town sheriff had yet to notice us. He cranked the pedals of his bike, pulled some tools out of his bag, and tried to wrestle his chain back on the sprocket wheel. He was having a hard time. He looked down at his dirty fingers and rubbed them together. Then he saw me. Fifty meters away: a boy with a giant pumpkin. What was I supposed to do? He could see that I was walking in his direction, so I just kept going. The pumpkin belonged to me, after all. My legs began to tremble, but it seemed to have been the right decision: The town sheriff's gaze returned to his bike. Then he looked up again and saw Tschick. Tschick had just gotten to the car, had thrown his bag of groceries in the backseat, and was about to climb into the driver's seat. The policeman stopped rubbing his hands together. He stared in Tschick's direction, took a step toward the car, then stopped again. There's nothing inherently suspicious about a boy getting into a car. Even when he opens the driver's door. But if Tschick were to start the engine, I knew what would happen next. I had to do something. I lifted the pumpkin up above my head and yelled, "Don't forget to bring the sleeping bag!"

I couldn't think of anything better. The policeman turned back to me. Tschick turned to me too. "Dad says to bring the sleeping bag! The sleeping bag!" I yelled again. When the cop turned again toward Tschick, I gestured at my head and my hip — meant to be a policeman's hat and gun — to try to telegraph the man's profession to Tschick. Without his hat on, and in those green cycling pants, it wasn't easy to tell. I must have looked like an idiot, but I couldn't think of any other way to signal that it was a cop. Tschick seemed to understand what was going on. He disappeared into the car and came out again with a sleeping bag in his hands. Then he closed the door and pretended to lock it (Dad gave me the keys, I just had to grab something), and came back toward me and the policeman with the sleeping bag. But he stopped after about ten steps. I wasn't a hundred percent sure why he stopped. But I think something in the cop's facial expression must have given away the fact that our clever move wasn't the greatest piece of acting he'd ever seen.

Tschick started backing up. Then he started to run. The policeman ran after him, but Tschick was already at the wheel. He backed onto the street at lighting speed and the policeman accelerated like a track star. Not because he could catch the car — there was no way he'd be able to do that — but so he could read the license plate number. Holy shit. A town sheriff who could run like a gold medalist. I stood there the whole time like an idiot, pumpkin in hand. As the Lada headed for the horizon, the sheriff finally turned back toward me. Don't ask what I did next. Normally, with any thought at all, I would never have done it. But nothing was normal anymore, and maybe it wasn't so stupid anyway. I ran to the cop's bicycle. I threw the pumpkin down and ran to the bike. I was significantly closer to it than he was at this point. I flipped it right side up and climbed onto the seat. The cop yelled, but fortunately he was yelling from a fair distance. I stepped on the pedal. Up to that second it had all been a blur, but now it became a vivid nightmare. I stepped with all my might on the pedal and didn't budge. It must have been in the highest gear, and I couldn't find the shifter. His shouts were getting closer. I had tears in my eyes and my thighs felt as if they were going to explode. But just as it seemed he would be able to reach out and grab me, I got the bike going and sped away from him.

CHAPTER TWENTY SEVEN

I flew through the village on its cobblestone roads. It didn't take me longer than a minute and a half to reach the town square, but I knew how risky it was since the cop had probably already gotten to a phone. If he wasn't stupid — and he didn't give any indication of being stupid — he would have called someone who could grab me as I sped through the center of town. Maybe there was more than one policeman in this village. I raced between gray houses and around corners and finally onto a path that led out into the fields.

As it started to get dark, I lay in the woods alone, wheezing and anxious. The policeman's bike was hidden under some dense brush. I wracked my brain as I waited. I was more and more unsure of what to do. I was a hundred or maybe two hundred kilometers south or southeast of Berlin in some forest, while Tschick was driving around somewhere in a light blue Lada with Munich plates on it, a car every cop in the area was on the lookout for, and I had no idea how we were going to find each other. Normally I guess you'd try to meet up where you'd lost each other. But that wouldn't work in this case — it was right in front of the town sheriff's place.

Another possibility would have been to go to Friedemann's

house and leave a message for Tschick. Or hope that he had left one for me. But for whatever reason, it seemed highly unlikely that he would have done that. The village was small, the people all knew each other, and Tschick would never have driven through town again in the Lada. The only chance was that he would try to sneak into town after nightfall, but even that was risky given the probability that everyone there had already heard about the whole thing. It also seemed unlikely to me because all of a sudden I thought of something much more likely.

If you couldn't meet where you'd last seen each other, you could still meet in the last *safe* place you'd been together — the observation platform, the snack stand, and the spot hidden by the elderberry bush.

It seemed somehow logical. At least it seemed logical as I lay there with my face in the muck. It was the easiest solution, and the more I thought about it the more convinced I was that it would occur to Tschick too. Because it occurred to me. And besides, the platform was in a good location — far enough away from town but close enough for me to reach by bike. Tschick must have seen me take off on the bike. So I cowered in the bushes through the night and then started off at first light. I rode way out around the village, going through the woods and fields. It wasn't hard to find my way, but it was much farther than I'd thought. I could see the ridgeline shrouded in fog in the distance, but it never seemed to get any closer. It didn't take long before I was extremely thirsty. And hungry. Off to the right of the field I was in, there were a few houses clustered around a little brick church, so I headed that way. The "village" consisted of three houses and a bus stop. The street signs were in a foreign language and I thought for a second I was already in the Czech Republic. But that was impossible. I hadn't seen anything like a border.

There was a funny little shop, but it was closed and didn't look like it was going to open up anytime soon. The shop windows were so dirty that they were practically opaque, but inside I could see half a loaf of bread and a faded pack of gum on a table, and behind that a shelf stacked with East German laundry detergent.

There was a crazy guy standing at the bus stop. He was pissing in the middle of the street, tottering around with his dick in his hand like he was having a grand old time. There was nobody else around, and the angled rays of the morning sun made the cobblestones of the road look as if they were coated with red enamel. I thought about ringing one of the doorbells and asking whoever answered to sell me something. But once I actually rang the bell at a house where a light was on — the name on the door was Lentz, I remember that clearly — I lost my nerve and just asked the man who opened the door if I could have a glass of water. The man was half-naked. He was wearing gym shorts and was sweating. He was young and clearly worked out, and had bandages on his wrists. "A glass of water!" he bellowed. He stared at me for a second and then pointed to a faucet on the side of the house. As I drank from the faucet he asked if I was okay. I told him I was doing a bike tour. He laughed and shook his head and asked again if everything was okay. I pointed to his bandages and asked if everything was okay with him. He suddenly got very serious, nodded, and the conversation was over.

When I arrived at the observation platform, I was alone atop the mountain and it was still early in the morning. Behind the sawmill I'd seen only a lone black car, and the snack stand up here was still covered by a locked grate. I walked down to the elderberry bush. Our garbage was still on the ground, but there was no sign of Tschick. I was incredibly disappointed.

For hour after hour, I sat up there and waited. And I got more and more distraught. People came and went, and tour buses came and went, but the Lada never appeared. It didn't seem like a good idea to ride anywhere else. If Tschick was driving around, he needed to be able to find me someplace. If we both ended up driving around, we'd never find each other. At some point I became convinced they must have caught him, and I resigned myself to spending the night under the elderberry bush. But then my gaze fell on a garbage can. It was filled with candy bar wrappers, empty beer bottles, and wine corks, and it occurred to me that we too had thrown away all of our trash in that very garbage can. We hadn't left anything under the elderberry bush. I ran like a madman back down to the bush — and found an empty Coke bottle. Looking at it more closely, I discovered a rolled-up note crammed into the neck of the bottle. I pulled it out and it read, *I'm in the bakery where we ran into Heckel. Come at six. — T* But that had been crossed out and another message was written beneath it: *Count Tschickula is working at the sawmill. Stay here and I'll pick you up at sunset.*

I sat happily at the observation platform until evening. Then I got more and more upset. Because Tschick didn't show up. There were no more tourists either, just a black car driving around in circles at the back of the parking lot. It had been there since dusk, and I'm not sure how blind you can be — because it wasn't until the car pulled right up to the platform and a man with a Hitler mustache opened the door that I realized it was a Lada. Our Lada.

I hugged Tschick, then punched him, then hugged him again. I couldn't calm down.

"Man!" I shouted. "Man, oh, man!"

"How do you like the color?" Tschick asked. Then we barreled down the hill with the pedal to the metal.

I told him everything that had happened to me since we'd lost each other. But what Tschick had to tell was much more interesting. As he was fleeing the scene he had accidentally come across the bakery where we'd met Heckel and had parked the car not far from there. He figured it was too risky to keep driving around. He sat in front of the bakery for the entire day and had seen nothing but police cars go by.

Then he'd walked to the observation platform, which was only a few kilometers away. He had waited for me there. But since I didn't show up — as I was sleeping in the woods — he left the note in the bottle about the bakery and went back to the car. On the way he'd passed a home improvement store and stolen masking tape and a case of spray cans. Since he hadn't seen any more cops on the street, he had put the spray paint in the car and driven back to the observation platform. But I still wasn't there, so he left the second note and parked the car at the sawmill and painted it. He had thought of everything: The car had new license plates now too.

When I told Tschick about the man with the bandages and the other one pissing in the street, he said he'd noticed that there were a lot of crazy people out here. As for the signs written in another language, he didn't know what the story was.

"It certainly isn't Russian," he said as we looked at a strange sign lit up by the first few streetlights to blink on.

The next day we were back on the autobahn. And this time not
by accident. We were feeling confident, we wanted to make
headway, and we did. For about fifty kilometers. Then Tschick
pointed to the fuel gauge, which was already well into the red.

"Shit," he said.

We hadn't thought about the fact that we would need to
get gas. At first it didn't seem like a huge problem. There was
a rest stop two kilometers up the road and we had money. But
then I realized that two eighth graders in a car might not look
right to the gas station employees. I should have realized that
before.

"Here's fifty, keep the change!" said Tschick, laughing
hysterically.

We pulled off at the rest stop anyway. It was shortly before
noon and the place was jammed. Tschick pulled past the diesel
pumps and parked between two tractor-trailers where nobody
could see us. We looked around sadly. Tschick said we'd never
be able to get gas there, and I suggested we use the tennis ball
to grab a different car.

"Too many people around," said Tschick.

"We'll just wait until it's less busy."

"Let's just wait until evening," he said. "Then one of us can go to the farthest pump and get it all ready, and the other can pull the Lada around on the outside — fill it up and go. That way we'll save money too."

Tschick thought it was a brilliant plan — as good as Hannibal marching over the Alps. And I might have agreed with him if I had known how a gas pump worked. But I'd never held a gas pump in my hand, and eventually I realized that he never had either. There's not only a trigger in the handle of the pump but some other lever to lock it or something. I'd seen my father do it a million times, but I never paid close attention.

We bought ice cream bars at the rest-stop shop, sat down on the curb opposite the pumps, and watched people fill up their tanks. It didn't look so difficult. It just took forever to fill up. And there were always people standing around, and an attendant watching everything from the panoramic window of his booth. Of course, we could have just put a few liters in and sped off, but then we'd be in the same jam by the time we reached the next rest stop.

"Don't you still have the tennis ball?" I asked. I pointed at the parking lot — so many nice cars.

"We can't steal a new car every time we run out of gas."

"But you still have the ball, right?" I looked at Tschick. He had his arms wrapped around his knees and his head buried.

"Yeah, yeah, yeah," he said. But he said that we wanted to take the Lada back, and that we couldn't steal a hundred cars one after the next. I found this all very enlightening. But what if it meant the end of our trip?

A red Porsche pulled up to a gas pump and a young woman with sleek blond hair got out and grabbed the handle with pink-polished fingernails. And that's when it hit me — I knew how we could get gas. We just had to siphon it out of another car! It was easy, I told Tschick. All we needed was a hose. You stick that in the gas tank, suck on it for a second, and the gas flows right out. I'd seen it in a book I got as a present when I started school. It was a book that explained the entire world — for six-year-olds. Obviously six-year-olds aren't taught how to steal gasoline. But I remembered an illustration of a bucket on top of a table. There was water in the bucket, and the water was flowing smoothly up and out of the rim of the bucket in a hose. It works because of some physics principle.

"What are you telling me? That the water flows up?"

"You have to suck on it to get it started."

"Haven't you ever heard of gravity? It won't flow up."

"It runs down once it gets started. Overall it's flowing downward."

"But the gas doesn't know that it will eventually be flowing downward."

"It's a law of physics. There's a name for it. Something with force and tube. The something-force rule."

"Bullcrap," said Tschick. "The bullcrap-sandwich rule, more like."

"Haven't you ever seen it in a movie?"

"Yeah, but that's *in a movie.*"

"I know it from a book," I said. I didn't say it was a book for six-year-olds. "I think the name is something with a C — like capital force or whatever."

"Capital crap, man."

"No, wait, that's not it. I know! Capillary! Capillary action is the name of the principle."

Tschick didn't say anything for a moment. He still didn't believe it. But the fact that I'd thought of the name of the force had taken the wind out of his sails. I told him that capillary action was strong enough to allow liquids to flow against gravity and all that. Mostly I kept at it just to make an effort — and because I didn't want our trip to be over. I mean, I'd never actually seen anyone do the trick with the hose.

We ate another round of ice cream bars and then another. And when we still didn't have a better idea, we decided to give it a try.

The problem, of course, was that we didn't have a hose. We looked all around the rest stop first, the area behind the gas station, the brush nearby, an adjacent field, and then farther and farther away. We found hubcaps, plastic tarps, bottles, loads of beer cans, and even a five-liter canister without a top. But nothing we could use as a hose. We looked for almost two hours, and while we did we cooked up all sorts of other plans for how we'd get out of there. But the plans got more and more ridiculous and that somehow made us more and more frustrated. No damn hose anywhere. No pipe, no tube, no cable. It was the kind of thing you always saw lying around when you didn't need one.

Tschick went into the rest-stop shop and looked in the auto parts section and anywhere else he thought he might find a hose of some sort. But there was nothing. Instead, he came out with a handful of drinking straws. We tried to connect the straws into a long tube, but with one glance at the rickety result even a brain-dead three-year-old could have seen it wasn't going to work.

And then Tschick had an idea. He remembered seeing a dump along the road. I couldn't remember seeing a dump, but

Tschick was sure. On the right-hand side of the road a few kilometers before the rest stop he'd seen giant mounds of garbage. And if there was a place we could definitely find a hose, that was it.

We took a dirt path that ran next to the guardrail alongside the highway, then cut through some woods and walked through fields and over fences, keeping the autobahn in view the whole time. It was just as hot as it had been the day before, and clouds of insects hung like fog at the edge of the woods. We walked for more than an hour without coming across the dump, and I was fed up and ready to ditch the idea of siphoning gas. But Tschick was completely convinced now that siphoning gas was the answer and didn't want to go back without a hose. While we were arguing, we came across a huge blackberry patch. And though most of the berries weren't ripe yet, there was a section that must have gotten more direct sun, because all the berries were ripe. And they tasted fantastic. I don't know if I've mentioned this, but there is nothing in the world I like better than blackberries. We stayed there for a while and gorged ourselves. Afterward it looked as if we were wearing makeup — our entire faces were purple.

I felt great again after that, and had no objection to walking another few hours in search of a hose. Which is good, because it did in fact take two hours before we caught sight of the dump. Giant mountains of garbage, hemmed in by the autobahn on one side and woods on the rest. We weren't the only ones poking around there. We could see an old man bent over collecting electrical wire. And there was a girl our age there too, covered in filth. And two children. But they didn't seem to be together.

I started working through a mound of household trash and picked up two photo albums to show Tschick. One was a family album full of pictures of a father, mother, son, and dog all smiling in every picture, even the dog. I flipped through it, then decided to throw it away after all — it made me depressed. It made me think of my mother and how badly things were going for her and how much more distress I was probably going to cause her when she found out about all of this. Then I slipped on a slick plank of wood and fell into a pile of rotten fruit.

Tschick had climbed onto another mound and found a big brown plastic canister with a filler cap. He beat the canister like a drum and then held it over his head. It was great. But as for a hose — negative.

I kept an eye out for washing machines, but in all the ones I found, the drum had been ripped out and the hose removed. As the hunched man wandered past me, I asked him if he had any idea why the hoses were missing from all the washing machines. He barely looked up and just pointed to his ears, as if he were deaf. The girl shot past me like a quick little animal at one point too, but she didn't even look at me. She was barefoot and her legs were blackened with dirt all the way up to her knees. She had on rolled-up army pants and a filthy T-shirt. She had small eyes, bulging lips, and a flat nose. And her hair — it looked like the clippers had gotten fouled up while she was having a haircut. I decided not to try to talk to her. She had a wooden box under her arm, but I wasn't sure if she'd

143

found it here or had brought it to carry things, and it wasn't clear what she was looking for anyway.

After a while I went up and met Tschick on top of the biggest mound. Neither of us had found anything except for the ten-liter canister Tschick had. But what use was that? This was a dump with no hoses. We sat down on a gutted washing machine on top of the mountain of garbage. The sagging sun had already reached the tops of the trees. The sound of the autobahn was quieter, and the old man and the children were no longer in sight. The only person left was the girl, who sat on top of another mound looking across at us. Her legs hung from the open door of an old wardrobe. She yelled something in our direction.

"What?" I yelled back.

"You're idiots!" she called.

"Are you crazy or something?"

"You heard me, moron. Your friend's an idiot too!"

"What the hell kind of asshole is that?" said Tschick.

For a long time all we could see were her legs, dangling out of the wardrobe. Then she sat up and started to put on a pair of boots that were sitting next to her in a drawer. She looked across at us.

"I've got something!" she yelled, though it was clear she didn't mean the boots. "Do you?"

"Shove it up your ass!" shouted Tschick.

She stopped tying the boots for a second. Then she bent forward and stretched out her legs and called, "You're so dumb you couldn't even fuck!"

"Shove it up your ass and shut your mouth!"

"Russian bastard!" She'd made out his accent.

"I'm going to come over there!"

"Oooh, the big bad man is going to come over here. What are you going to do? Come on! Come over here, you pussy! I'm *so* scared."

"I don't think she's right in the head," said Tschick.

The mounds were so steep that it would have taken several minutes to get over there.

It was quiet for a few minutes, and then she called, "What were you looking for?"

"A pile of shit," said Tschick.

"Hoses!" I shouted. All the cursing was beginning to bug me. "We were looking for hoses. You?"

A crow swooped over the mound and skidded down on a piece of sheet metal. The girl didn't answer. She lay back down in the wardrobe again.

"What about you?" I shouted.

For a while all you could see were her filthy calves. Then a hand came into view.

"Hoses are over there."

"What?"

"Over there."

"She's just pretending she knows," said Tschick.

"I heard that!" yelled the girl.

"So?"

"Dirty bastard!"

"Where over there?" I called.

"Where am I pointing?"

You could see her knee and her hand, but to be honest it looked as if her hand was pointing at the sky. It was quiet for a few minutes. Then I climbed down from our mound and up the one she was on.

"Where?" I asked, catching my breath as I approached her wardrobe.

She lay there without moving and stared at my neck. "Come here. Come on."

"Where?" I said, and suddenly she hopped up. Surprised, I staggered back a few steps and nearly fell. Behind me was a ten-foot drop. "Do you know where the hoses are or not?"

"You're the queer with the dirty Russian boyfriend, yeah?" She wiped a piece of fruit off my shirt that I hadn't noticed. Then she picked up her wooden box, tucked it under her arm, and started off. Up the next mound, then the next, and then she stopped and pointed down, "There!"

At the foot of this mound was a smaller mound of scrap metal and behind it a huge pile of hoses. Long hoses, short hoses, all sorts of tubes and hoses. Tschick, who had followed us, had already scrambled down and grabbed a thick washing machine hose. "Built-in angle!" he called. He wouldn't look at the girl.

"No, an angle is no good," I said. I disconnected a hand-held showerhead from its hose.

"What do you need it for?"

"An angle is always good," said Tschick, running the angled end into his canister.

"Hey, I asked you something," said the girl.

"What was the question?"

"What do you want it for?"

"It's a birthday present for my father."

Oddly enough she didn't curse at me. She just put an annoyed look on her face and said, "I showed you where the crap was, so now you can tell me what you want it for."

Tschick was kneeling among the hoses, examining the various washing machine hoses and shoving them into the canister.

"Why do you want them?"

"We stole a car," said Tschick. "And now we need to steal gasoline for it."

He looked at the girl through a big tube.

She pelted him with about a hundred curse words. "I should have known. You retards. Even though I showed you the damn things. Typical. Do whatever you want." She wiped her face with her T-shirt and sat down with her wooden box on a tractor tire. I held up my shower hose and gave Tschick the signal to quit looking. With three hoses and a canister we headed off.

"What are you really going to do with them?" the girl yelled.

"You're getting on my nerves," Tschick said.

"Do you have anything to eat?"

"Do we look like we do?"

"You look like retards."

"You're repeating yourself."

"Do you have any money?"

"For you?"

"You wouldn't have found them without me."

"Go fuck yourself."

Tschick and the girl continued to insult each other until we were nearly out of earshot. He kept turning around and yelling insults at her, and she shouted insults back at him from a mound of garbage. I stayed out of it.

But then she started to run after us. For some reason I had a funny feeling about the whole thing when I saw *how* she was running after us. Normally, girls don't run right — they run awkwardly. But this girl could *run*. She ran like it was a matter of life or death — and with the wooden box under her arm no less. I wasn't exactly afraid of her, the way she hurtled toward us, but I definitely thought she was weird.

"I'm hungry," she said, catching her breath. She was looking at us as if she was staring into the distance.

"There are blackberries over there," I said.

She drew a circle around her mouth with her finger and said, "And here I was thinking you were queer. Because of the lipstick."

Tschick and I walked on, and he whispered to me that she wasn't right in the head.

We hadn't gotten far when we heard her yelling again.

"Hey!" she called.

"What?"

"Where are the blackberries, man? Where are the blackberries?"

CHAPTER THIRTY

The way back seemed to go a lot faster than the way there. Maybe it was because the girl talked nonstop. At first she had walked behind us, then between us, and then on the other side of the path. Tschick held his nose at some point and looked at me, and it was true. She stank. She smelled horrible. You didn't notice it while in the dump, because the whole place stank. But she was giving off a serious stench. If she'd been in a cartoon, flies would have been buzzing around her head. And she talked nonstop. I don't remember exactly what she was talking about, but she kept asking us stuff like where we lived and where we went to school, whether we were good at math. That seemed particularly important to her — whether we were good at math. She asked if we had siblings, whether we knew Cantor's theorem of infinity and on and on. But whenever we asked why she wanted to know all of this, she never answered. She wouldn't even tell us what she was looking for at the dump.

Instead, she told us that she wanted to work at a TV station one day. Her dream was to be the host of a quiz show. "Because you look good and you work with words." She had a cousin who worked in TV and said it was a super job except that you had to work nights.

After she'd talked for long enough about TV, she came back to the joke about us stealing a car and said that Tschick was a funny guy, and that she had laughed inside when he'd told the joke about stealing the car. Tschick scratched his head and said that, yeah, she was right, he was a funny guy sometimes, which was exactly why he planned to give his father a hose for his birthday.

"And you're more the quiet type," said the girl, poking me in the shoulder and asking me again if I *really* went to school. I hope we reach the blackberries soon, I thought, or we'll never get rid of her.

I figured she would turn around and go back at some stage, but she walked the three or four kilometers to the blackberry patch. I was hungry again too, and so was Tschick, so we all plunged into the berry patch.

"We have to get rid of her somehow," whispered Tschick. I looked at him as if he had said we shouldn't saw off our feet.

Then the girl started to sing. Very quietly at first, in English, broken by pauses when she was chewing berries.

"Now she's singing some crap too," said Tschick. I said nothing, because for one thing she wasn't singing crap. She was singing "Survivor" by Destiny's Child. Her pronunciation was ridiculous. She must not have spoken English — it sounded as if she was just imitating the sounds. But she sang unbelievably well. I gingerly grabbed a thorny branch with my thumb and pointer finger and pulled it aside to have a look through the leaves at the girl singing and humming and munching berries there in the bushes. Add to that the taste of the blackberries in my own mouth, the orange-red sunset, and the background sound of the autobahn, and I found myself in an extremely weird mood.

"We're going to head off on our own now," said Tschick when we were standing on the path again.

"Why?"

"We have to get home."

"I'll go with you. I'm going that way too," said the girl.

And Tschick said, "This isn't the way you were going."

He told her a thousand times that we didn't want her to come with us, but she just shrugged her shoulders and kept walking along behind us. Finally Tschick faced her and said, "Do you know how bad you stink? You smell like a pile of crap. Get out of here."

As we walked on, I could tell she was still following us. But she started walking slower and slower, and soon enough we could no longer see her. Darkness started to creep between the trees. We heard some noise in the bushes at one point, but it was probably just an animal.

"If she follows us, we're screwed," said Tschick.

Just to be safe, we walked faster and then, after rounding a sharp turn, hid in some bushes and waited. We waited at least five minutes, and when the girl didn't appear, we walked the rest of the way back to the rest stop.

"You didn't have to say all that stuff about her smelling bad."

"I had to say something. And anyway, man, she did stink! She must live in that dump."

"She sure did sing nicely," I said after a while. "And there's no way she lives in the dump."

151

"Why did she ask us for food?"

"Yeah, okay, but this isn't Romania. People don't live in dumps here."

"Did you catch a whiff of her?"

"We probably smell just as bad."

"I'm telling you, she lives there. Ran away from home. Seriously, I know people like that. She's messed up. Nice body and all, but she's a homeless nut-job."

To the left, above the autobahn, you could see the first stars. It was getting tough to see the path and stay on it. I suggested we walk along the shoulder of the autobahn. I was afraid we'd lose our way otherwise. It was a stupid argument since we could hear the rush of the autobahn from the woods anyway. But to be honest, I was getting a little afraid in the dark woods. I have no idea why. It couldn't have been the fear of running into criminals — we were definitely the only criminals running around in those woods. In fact, maybe that's what made me uncomfortable. I guess I finally realized that's what we were. I was happy when we could see the neon lights of the rest stop through the trees.

The first thing we did was buy ice cream and Cokes. We hid the canister behind a guardrail and walked through the parking lot with our ice creams, eyeballing the gas tanks of parked cars. None of them could be opened. I was beginning to have doubts when Tschick finally found an old VW Golf with a broken gas tank door.

We waited until it was really dark and nobody was anywhere in sight, and then got to work.

The washing machine hose was so inflexible that we might as well have thrown it out. But we got the shower hose into the tank with no problem. We just couldn't get the gas to start flowing. Even though the tank was full. The end of the hose was all wet with gasoline.

After I'd tried sucking on the tube about ten times with no luck, Tschick tried. After he'd sucked a bunch of times he looked at me and said, "What the hell kind of book was it you saw this in? Where'd you get it?"

I had no desire to tell him what kind of book it was. I tried sucking on the tube again. I could tell the gas was coming up the tube. Once I had it almost to my lips. But no more than three drops came out. We squatted between the parked cars and looked at each other.

"I know how it works," Tschick finally said. "Fill your mouth and then spit it out. That'll work for sure."

"Why me?"

"This wasn't my idea."

"I have a better idea. Do you still have the tennis ball?"

"Oh, man," said Tschick. "I can't. No way."

"It's pitch-black out here. Nobody will see us."

"I *can't*," Tschick said with a pained look on his face. "You didn't really believe that, did you? You can't open a car lock with a tennis ball. Otherwise everybody would steal cars. The Lada was open the whole time. Didn't you notice? The lock is busted or maybe the owner just never locks it — I mean, who's going to steal a rust bucket like that anyway. My brother realized it was always open and . . . don't look at me like that! My brother pulled the same prank on me with the tennis ball. Oh, man. *Don't turn around.*"

"What's wrong?"

"Get your head down. There's somebody over there. By the Dumpsters."

I leaned up against the Golf and tried to carefully look over my shoulder.

"They're gone. There was a shadow over there by the recycling bin."

"So let's get out of here."

"There he is again. I'll have a smoke."

"What?"

"Camouflage."

"Forget camouflage, let's get out of here."

Tschick stood up and kicked the container and hose under the Golf. It made a loud scraping noise. I stood up too. Something moved behind the Dumpsters. I saw it out of the corner of my eye.

"Could be goats," murmured Tschick. He lit up a cigarette in his mouth, standing right next to the gas tank door.

"Why don't you just throw a match in there while you're at it."

He took a few puffs and started stretching. It was the least convincing acting job of all time.

Then we went slowly back to the Lada. As we walked away I nudged the gas tank door of the VW closed with my hip.

"You idiots!" yelled someone behind us.

We looked into the darkness in the direction the voice had come from.

"Screwing around for half an hour without getting a drop. Idiots. Real pros."

"Maybe you can say it a little louder," said Tschick.

"And smoking on top of it!"

"Can't you shout any louder? We want the whole parking lot to know."

"You guys are too dumb to fuck."

"True. And now could you please piss off?"

"Don't you know you have to suck on the hose?"

"What do you think we were doing the whole time? Get out of here!"

"Shhh!" I said.

Tschick and I ducked behind a car. The girl didn't care. She looked around the parking lot.

"There's nobody around, you scaredy-cats. Where's the hose?"

She took our equipment out from under the VW. She stuck one end of the hose into the gas tank and the other — along with a finger — into her mouth. She sucked ten, fifteen times like she was gulping down the air; then she pulled the hose out of her mouth with her finger over the end.

"Right. Where's the canister?"

I pulled it out from under the car and set it down. She stuck the hose into the mouth of the container and gas rushed out of the tank. All by itself. And it didn't stop.

"Why didn't it work for us?" asked Tschick.

"The end of the hose has to be below the level of the gas in the car," said the girl.

"Aha," I said.

"Oh," said Tschick. We watched as the canister filled up. The girl kneeled down, and when the flow of gas stopped, she screwed the gas cap back on and shut the tank door.

"Below what level?" whispered Tschick.

"Ask her, you idiot," I said.

That's how we met Isa. With her elbows on the backs of the two front seats she watched closely as Tschick started the Lada. We still had no desire to take her along, but after the whole gasoline thing it would have been tough not to. She wanted to come with us, and when she heard we were from Berlin she said that was exactly where she was heading. And then when we explained that we weren't going toward Berlin right now, she said that was perfect. She kept trying to find out where we were going, but since she wouldn't tell us where she was going, we didn't tell her either. We just said we were heading south, at which point she remembered she had a half-sister in Prague she really needed to go see. And we had to go right past Prague anyway. Plus, like I said, it would have been tough not to take her with us since she was the only reason we had any gas.

Once we were rolling down the autobahn again, we opened all the windows. It still stank, just not as badly. Tschick had adapted to driving on the autobahn by this point. He drove like Hitler in his heyday, and Isa sat in back and jabbered on and on. She was suddenly full of energy and shook the backs of our seats as she talked. Not that it was normal behavior, but it

was preferable to the streams of obscenities she'd been screaming earlier. And the things she talked about weren't entirely
uninteresting. I mean, she wasn't stupid. And even Tschick
held his tongue after a while and nodded as he listened to her.

But the two of them still hadn't entirely settled their differ-
ences. When Isa stuck her head between the front seats Tschick
motioned to her hair and said, "There's things living in there."

Isa sat back immediately and said, "I know." And a few
kilometers later she asked, "Do you guys happen to have a pair
of scissors? I need to cut my hair."

With the help of the exit signs, we tried to figure out where
we were. But none of us recognized the names of the towns. I
began to suspect we hadn't gotten far on all those dinky country roads. But it didn't matter. At least not to me. The autobahn
didn't seem to be heading south anymore, and at some point
we exited and started following the sun along country roads
again.

Isa asked to hear our lone cassette tape. Then after one
song, she asked us to throw it out the window. A ridge of
mountains came into view on the horizon — we were heading
straight for them. They were really tall, with jagged bare tops.
We had no idea what mountain range it could be. There was
no sign. Definitely not the Alps. Were we still in Germany?
Tschick swore there were no mountains in East Germany. Isa
said there were, but the tallest were only a thousand meters
high. In geography, we'd just studied Africa. Before that we'd
learned about America, and before that the Balkans. We hadn't
gotten any closer to Germany than that. And now, here was a
mountain range that wasn't supposed to be there. At least we
all agreed it didn't belong there. It took about half an hour

before we reached the foot of the mountains, and then we began the serpentine climb up them.

We had sought out the dinkiest road we could find, and we had to put the Lada in first gear and fight our way up. To our left and right the fields hung like towels from the steep hillsides. Then came a forest. And when we emerged from the forest we were sitting at the top of a gorge with a crystal clear lake in it. A small lake. Half of it was bordered by pale gray cliffs, with a concrete and metal structure on one side. The rest was ringed by a dike of some sort. And we were the only people around. We drove down and parked the car near the edge of the lake. From the concrete dam you could look down toward the valley below and across at the rest of the mountains. A few hundred meters below the dam was a little village. This was an ideal spot to spend the night.

The lake looked too cold for swimming. I stood on the dam next to Isa and took a deep breath. Tschick went over to the car, grabbed something, and walked back with it casually hidden behind him. We'd apparently both had the same thought. With a nod from Tschick, we picked Isa up and tossed her into the water. A fountain of water shot up as she went under, and another one shot up as she surfaced with her arms flailing. It was at that moment that I realized we had no idea if she could swim. She screamed and splashed — though she overdid it enough that you could tell she knew how to swim. She also started treading water and wasn't sinking an inch. She shook her wet hair, swam a little breaststroke, and cursed us out. Tschick threw her the bottle of shower gel he'd gotten from the car. And as I was trying to figure out if that was funny or if I should feel bad for her, I got a poke in the back and fell into the water too. It was colder than cold. I screamed as soon as my head was out of the water. Tschick stood on the side and laughed as Isa alternately laughed and cursed.

The concrete structure was too tall to climb up, so we had to swim across the lake to a part where the bank was at water level. While we swam, Isa let an unending stream of curses fly, kicked me underwater, and said that I was an even bigger moron than my boyfriend. We got into a tussle. As this was going on, Tschick strolled to the car, put on his bathing suit, and came to the lakeside with a cigarette in his mouth and a towel over his shoulder.

"This is how a gentleman goes swimming," he said, making what was supposed to be an elegant face. Then he dove headfirst into the lake.

We cursed him in tandem.

When we got back on land, Isa immediately took off her shirt and pants and everything else and began to soap herself up. That was just about the last thing I had expected.

"Lovely," she said. She was standing in knee-deep water, gazing out at the landscape, and washing her hair. I wasn't sure where to look. I acted like I was looking all around. She really did have a great body and her skin was covered with goose bumps. I had goose bumps too. Tschick swam to the bank freestyle, and oddly enough there was no more chitchat. Nobody said anything, nobody cursed, and nobody made any jokes. We just washed ourselves, shivered from the cold, and dried ourselves off with the same towel.

With a mountain view and fog beginning to creep into the valley below, we ate a package of gummy bears we had left over from our visit to the supermarket. Isa had on one of my

T-shirts and shiny Adidas shorts. Her stinky clothes were lying on the edge of the dike — and stayed there, forever.

That night we tried to figure out where she was from and where she was trying to go, but the only thing we could get out of her were crazy stories. It was clear she wouldn't tell us what she was doing in the dump or what she had in her wooden box even to save her own life. The only thing she told us was her last name, Schmidt. Isa Schmidt. At least, that was the only thing she told us that we believed.

Early the next morning, Tschick set off alone to go buy food in the village down in the valley. I was still half-asleep on the air mattress, looking out over the dimly lit landscape. Isa had the back of the Lada open and asked again if we happened to have scissors and if I would cut her hair.

I did find a little pair of scissors in the first aid kit, but I'd never cut hair before. She didn't care, and she wanted it all cut off except for a row of bangs in front. She sat down on the side of the dike, took off her T-shirt, and said, "Go ahead."

After a few seconds she turned to me and said, "Why haven't you started? I don't want the T-shirt to get covered in hair."

So I started cutting. At first I tried not to touch her head too much while I was cutting her hair, but it's difficult to give someone a haircut with tiny scissors without bracing yourself on their head. And it's even more difficult not to keep looking at naked breasts when they're right in front of you.

"Look, he's jacking off," said Isa. I looked toward the edge of the woods and saw an old man standing there — not even behind a tree — with his pants around his ankles spanking it.

"Oh, man," I said, taking the scissors away from her head.

Isa jumped up, picked up some rocks, and, with lightning speed, started running toward the old man. She shot up the hill and started throwing rocks as she ran. She was throwing the rocks fifty meters, easy — and dead straight, like laser beams. And somehow it didn't surprise me. Anyone who could run like her could obviously throw well too. At first the old man kept stroking, but when Isa got a bit closer he whipped up his pants and staggered into the woods. Isa followed him, yelling and waving her arms wildly. But I could see that she had stopped throwing rocks. When she reached the edge of the woods she stopped. She came back out of breath and sat down in the exact same spot as before.

I must have stood there like a statue for a while because at some point she tapped my thigh and said, "Go on."

The only thing missing was the bangs. I kneeled in front of Isa to be able to make a straight line. And I gave it everything I had to avoid taking even the tiniest glimpse anywhere except at her forehead. I held the scissors perfectly level and made a tentative initial trim. Then I leaned back and surveyed it like a real artist and cut a bit more. The hair fell past her small eyes and on down.

"It doesn't have to be perfect," Isa said. "The rest of it's a mess anyway."

"Not at all. It looks great," I said. And in my mind, *You look great*.

I didn't say anything more. When I was done, Isa wiped the hair away and we sat next to each other on the dike, looked out at the view, and waited for Tschick to come back. Isa still hadn't put her T-shirt back on. In front of us the mountains were still shrouded in a bluish morning mist that also hung in the valleys. I asked myself why it was so beautiful. I wanted to say how beautiful it was, or how beautiful I thought it was and why — or rather, how beautiful it was and that I couldn't explain why it was so beautiful. But at some point I figured it wasn't necessary to explain.

"Have you ever had sex?" asked Isa.

"What?"

"You heard me."

She had put her hand on my knee and my face felt as if someone had thrown boiling water on it.

"No," I said.

"Well?"

"Well what?"

"Do you want to?"

"Do I want to what?"

"You understand what I'm saying."

"No," I said.

My voice was suddenly high and squeaky. After a bit Isa took her hand away and we sat silently for at least ten minutes. There was still no sign of Tschick. Suddenly the mountains and the view seemed totally uninteresting. What had Isa just said? What had I answered? It was only a few words — what did they mean? My mind was racing, and it would take five hundred pages to write down all the thoughts that went through my head in the next five minutes. I'm sure none of it was too fascinating anyway — it's only fascinating in the moment, when you're in a situation like that. I kept asking myself whether Isa was serious. And whether I was serious when I said I didn't want to sleep with her, if that really was what I'd said. Though it was true that I didn't want to sleep with her. I mean, I thought she was amazing and all, but at that moment, on that misty morning, I thought it was perfect just sitting there next to her with her hand on my knee. And it was incredibly disappointing when she took her hand away. It took an eternity before I was able to form a sentence. I practiced saying it in my head about ten times and then said it aloud in a voice that made it sound as if I were about to have a heart attack. "But I like having your . . . um, uh . . . hand on my knee."

"Oh yeah?"

"Yeah."

"Why?"

My God. Why? Another heart attack.

Isa put her arm around my shoulder.

"You're shivering," she said.

"I know," I said.

"You don't know much."

"I know."

"We could kiss. If you'd like."

And at that exact moment, Tschick came into view carrying two bags from a bakery. There was no kissing.

Instead, we went up the mountain. We had never planned out what we wanted to do, but as we ate breakfast we kept looking around at a mountain that looked like the tallest mountain on earth. At some point it became obvious we had to go up it. The only question was how. Isa wanted to hike up. I agreed. But Tschick thought going on foot was absurd. "If you want to fly, you use an airplane," he said. "If you want to wash your clothes, you use a washing machine. And if you want to go up a mountain, you use a car. We're not in Bangladesh."

We drove through the woods toward the mountain, but it was difficult to figure out which turns to take. Only beyond the mountain did we find a road snaking its way toward the top, and we crept along cliffs until we reached a pass. From there the road went back down again, so we had to walk to the peak after all.

Either we were going up some route the tourists didn't use, or we were the only ones there that morning. In any event we didn't come across anyone except a few sheep and cows. It took two hours to reach the very top, but it was worth it. The view looked like a really great postcard. There was a giant wooden cross at the highest point, and below that a little cabin.

The entire cabin was covered with carvings. We sat down there and read some of the letters and numbers cut into the wood: CKH 4/23/61, SONNY '86, HARTMANN 1923.

The oldest one we could find was: ANSELM WAIL 1903. Old letters cut into old, dark wood. And then the view and the warm summer air and the scent of hay wafting up from the valleys below.

Tschick pulled out a pocketknife and started carving. As we talked and basked in the sun and watched Tschick carve, I kept thinking about the fact that in a hundred years we'd all be dead. Like Anselm Wail was dead. His family was all dead too. His parents were dead, his children were dead, everyone who ever knew him was dead. And if he ever made anything or built anything or left anything behind, it was probably dead as well — destroyed, blown away by two world wars — and the only thing left of Anselm Wail was his name carved in a piece of wood. Why had he carved it there? Maybe he'd been on a road trip, like us. Maybe he'd stolen a car or a carriage or a horse or whatever they had back then and rode around having fun. But whatever it was, it would never again be of interest to anyone because there was nothing left of his fun, of his life, of anything. The only people who would ever know anything at all about Anselm Wail were the people who climbed this mountain. And the same thing would be true of us. Suddenly I wished Tschick had carved our full names in the wood. Though it took him almost an hour just for the six letters and two numbers he did carve. He did a nice job, and when he was finished it said: AT MK IS '10.

"Everyone'll think we were here in 1910," said Isa. "Or 1810."

"I think it looks nice," I said.

"I like it too," said Tschick.

"And if some joker comes and carves a few letters in between it will say ATOMKRISE '10," said Isa. "The famous atomic crisis of 2010."

"Oh, shut up," said Tschick, but I thought it was pretty funny.

The fact that our initials were there with all the others — alongside initials carved by dead people — really did my head in.

"I don't know how you guys feel," I said, "but all the people here, the dates — I mean, death." I scratched my head and didn't know what to say. "I guess what I'm trying to say is that I think it's cool that we're here. I want you to know that I'm happy to be here with you. And that we're friends. But you never know how long — I mean, I don't know how long Facebook will exist, but I'd still like to know what becomes of you fifty years from now."

"Google us," said Isa.

"You can Google Isa Schmidt?" said Tschick. "Aren't there a hundred thousand of them?"

"I was going to suggest something different, actually," I said. "What do you say to meeting here again in fifty years? In this exact spot, in fifty years. On July 17, 2060, at five o'clock in the afternoon. Even if we haven't had any contact in thirty years. Everyone will come here, regardless of whether you're a manager at Bosch or living in Australia or whatever. Let's swear on it and then never mention it again. Or is that stupid?"

No, they didn't think it was stupid. We stood next to the carved initials and swore. And I bet we all thought about whether it was possible that we'd still be alive in fifty years and be back here. And wondered whether we'd be pathetic old people, though I didn't think that was possible. Figured it would probably be difficult for us to get up the mountain at that age. That we'd all have our own stupid cars, that inside we'd still be the same people, and that thoughts of Anselm Wail would still hit me like a ton of bricks, just as they had today.

"Let's do it," said Isa.

Tschick wanted us all to cut our fingers and daub blood on the initials, but Isa said we weren't Winnetou or whatever. So we didn't do it.

As we were walking back down we saw two soldiers below. At the pass, where we'd left the Lada, a couple of tour buses were parked. Isa ran over to one of them. The side of the bus had illegible writing on it, no idea what it said, but Isa went right up and started talking to the driver. Tschick and I watched from the Lada. Then Isa sprinted back and called, "Do you have thirty Euros? I can't pay you back right now, but I will sometime, I swear. My half-sister has money, and she owes me — and I need to go to her place."

I was speechless. Isa grabbed her wooden box out of the back of the car, looked at me and Tschick, cocked her head to one side and said, "I'll never make it there with you guys. Sorry."

She hugged Tschick; then she looked at me for a second, and then she hugged me and kissed me on the mouth. She turned and looked at the tour bus. The driver waved. I pulled thirty Euros out of my pocket and gave them to her silently. Isa hugged me again and ran toward the bus. "I'll get in touch! You'll get the money back!"

I knew I'd never see her again. Or at least not for fifty years.

"You didn't fall in love again, did you?" asked Tschick as he picked me up off the pavement. "Seriously, though, you have the touch with women."

The sun beat down and the asphalt looked like liquid metal as it receded into the distance. We were out of the mountains and were coming up on an intersection where cars were standing still. They looked as if they were quivering in the afternoon heat, like they were underwater. It didn't look like construction. More like an accident. And suddenly we saw a car with a flashing blue light on its roof.

Tschick swerved to the right and turned onto a road through a field lined with tall electrical transmission towers. The road was wide enough that a truck could have driven it, but it was grown over with grass and looked as if it hadn't been used in a long time. The police didn't seem to have noticed us. But we could see the police car for only a few more seconds before the road wound its way into a birch forest. There were birch saplings beneath the bigger birches so you couldn't see more than a few meters in any direction. The only place you could see anything was above, where the sky shone through the tops of the trees and transmission towers were visible now and then. The road kept getting narrower and didn't really give the impression that it was leading anywhere. It finally ended at a lopsided wooden gate hanging awkwardly from its hinges. Beyond the gate were marshy lowlands, and those marshy lowlands looked so different from the rest of the landscape that we looked at each other with the same thought: *Where on Earth are we?* We deliberated for a few minutes, and then I got out and yanked the gate open. Tschick drove through and I shut it again.

Flat mounds of light-colored earth were separated by dark swampy patches that were purplish green. And scattered in the swamps were concrete blocks with metal rods sticking out of them — and each rod had some kind of yellow flag on it. At first there were only a few of the concrete blocks, but the farther we drove, the more of them there were, until the entire landscape consisted of the blocks with yellow flags stuck in them. One every few meters as far as you could see. The Richard Clayderman tape would have been the perfect soundtrack because the view was just so tragic — like a sad tinkling piano. The road was getting swampy too, and Tschick crept along in first gear through soft potholes, the transmission towers always next to us. I was sweating. Four kilometers. Five. The terrain began to change, rising slightly. The row of transmission towers ended and the wires hung down from the last one like hair. Ten meters beyond, the world ended.

You had to have seen it: The landscape just stopped. We got out and stood by the last clump of grass. At our feet the ground had been steeply cut away, dropping at least thirty or forty meters down. And below was a moonscape. The ground was whitish gray and pockmarked with craters so big entire buildings could have fit in them. Off to our left was a bridge that led out over the abyss. Although bridge is probably not the right word. It was more like a trestle made out of wood and steel — like a giant scaffold running dead straight out across the pit to the other side, which was maybe two kilometers away. Maybe more. It was impossible to gauge the distance. You couldn't tell what was on the other side either. Maybe trees and shrubs, but who knew. Behind us the massive swamp, in front of us the void. And even if you listened closely, you heard absolutely nothing. No crickets, not a single blade of grass rustling, no wind, no flies, nothing.

We wracked our brains for a while trying to think what this place could be. Then we walked over to look at the trestle. It was wider than it looked from a distance, and was covered with thick wood planks. There didn't seem to be any other way around the abyss. And since we didn't want to drive back the way we'd come, Tschick went and got the Lada. He rolled a few meters onto the trestle — or bridge, or causeway, or whatever it was — and said, "It'll work."

Still, I didn't like the look of it. I got back in the car, and, even slower than a walking pace, we drove out along the wooden planks. The noise the planks made was so hollow and eerie that I got back out so I could walk ahead of the car. I kept an eye out for broken planks, tested suspicious looking spots with my feet, and looked through the cracks down into the depths. Tschick rolled along a few car lengths behind me. Anyone who had come upon us would have thought we looked like old people, creeping along. On the other hand, this wasn't exactly a street with an express lane.

When we had gotten far enough out that we could barely see the spot where we'd started but still couldn't really see the far side either, we took a break. Tschick grabbed Cokes out of the car and we sat on the edge of the plank road. Or tried to, anyway. The wood was so hot you couldn't sit on it until you stood there and cast a shadow for a while on the spot where you wanted to sit. We stared out at the crater landscape. And once I'd looked at the crater landscape for long enough, I thought about Berlin. It was suddenly difficult to imagine that I had once lived there. I could hardly imagine that I'd gone to school there. And I also couldn't possibly imagine that I would go back again.

On the other side of the abyss were scraggy bushes and some grass and a sort of village. A crumbling road meandered between derelict buildings. The windows were nearly all broken, the roofs caved in. No signs, no cars, no vending machines, nothing. The fences around the gardens had long since fallen apart. Weeds grew from every crack.

We went inside an abandoned farmhouse and looked through the rooms. Moldy wooden shelves leaned against one wall. In a kitchen, an empty jam jar and a plate. A newspaper from 1995 on the floor with a report on strip mining. Once we were sure there were no people in the entire area, we went through a few more houses. But we didn't find anything interesting. Old clothes hangers, worn out rubber boots, a couple of tables and chairs. I had expected at least one skeleton. Though we didn't venture down into the dark basements.

We drove on through the town. The windows of one two-story ruin had been covered with plywood, and someone had painted symbols and numbers in white paint on the wood. There were white symbols and numbers painted all over the place — on rocks to the left and right of the road, on fence posts. And then in the middle of the road a huge pile of scrap wood and planks. There were car tracks going around it, and as Tschick approached it warily, shifting down to first gear, we heard an incredible blast. Then a creaking sound. We looked at each other. The Lada was standing still now, and then came another blast that sounded like someone had taken a sledgehammer to the car's body panels. Or had thrown a big rock at it. Or shot at it. Tschick turned his head, and then we realized the entire back window was cracked in a spiderweb pattern.

I sprang out of the car. I don't know why, but I jumped into some grass behind the car. And I don't remember the next few seconds. What I do know — because Tschick told me afterward — is that he threw the car into reverse and shouted at me to get in. But I had crawled alongside the car and was waving both of my arms above the hood. I was also carefully peeking at the ruin on the opposite side of the road, scanning the bombed out windows until I saw just what I expected: In one of the window frames was somebody holding a rifle aimed at us. I looked at the muzzle for a second, but then he raised the barrel and put down the gun. It was an old man.

He was standing on the second floor of the house with white writing on it. He was shaking, but not, as far as I could tell, the same way I was shaking. In his case it looked to be old age making him shake. He put a hand up to shield his eyes against the blinding sun as I continued to wave like an idiot.

"What are you doing? Get in!" Tschick yelled. But I had stood up and started walking — still waving my arms and showing my hands — toward the building.

"We don't want anything! We just got lost. We're leaving!" I called to the old man.

He nodded. He picked up the rifle by the barrel, shook it in the air, and shouted, "No timetable! No map and no timetable!"

I stayed there in the yard in front of his house and tried to express with my body language how right he was.

"Never go into the field without a map!" he yelled. "Come on in. I have sodas. Come on in."

Obviously that was the last thing I wanted. To go in there. But he insisted. And in the end it wasn't a very difficult decision. He could easily still shoot us. It was tough getting around all the wood, but the old man didn't seem to be too crazy. I mean, at least he spoke like a normal person.

His living room — if you could call it that — wasn't in much better condition than the rooms we'd searched in other houses. You could tell it was occupied, but it was incredibly dark and dirty. A bunch of black-and-white photos hung on one wall.

We had to sit on a sofa and the old man, now apparently in a festive mood, brought a half-full bottle of Fanta orange soda. "Drink," he said. "Go ahead and drink out of the bottle."

He sat across from us in a comfy chair and started sipping some kind of moonshine out of an old jam jar. The rifle was between his knees. I had figured he'd ask us about the Lada first off, or ask where we were trying to get to. But it turned out he wasn't itching to know any of that stuff. As soon as he heard we were from Berlin, he was most interested in whether the city had really changed as much as they said, and whether you could walk on the street without being attacked. After we told him about ten times that violence was unheard of in our school, he suddenly asked, "Do you have sweethearts?"

I was going to say no, but Tschick answered more quickly.

"His is named Tatiana, and I'm crazy about Angelina," he said. I realized why he said it right away, but the answer didn't seem to satisfy the old man.

"Because you are two very handsome boys," he said.

"No, no," said Tschick.

"At your age, you don't know in a lot of cases which way you might lean."

"Nah," said Tschick, shaking his head. I shook my head too, sort of the way a Lionel Messi fan would shake his head if you asked him if he didn't really think Cristiano Ronaldo was the greatest soccer player of all time.

"So you guys are in love with these girls, yeah?"

We said yes. It made me kind of queasy the way he kept dancing around the topic. He just kept talking about girls and love and the fact that the most beautiful thing in the world was the alabaster body of adolescence.

"Believe me," he said. "One day you close your eyes and the next you open them to find withered flesh hanging in tatters. Love, love! Carpe diem."

He got up, took two steps over to the wall, and pointed at one of the many little photos. Tschick shot me a worried look, but I got up immediately, put on my best overly respectful smile, and examined the photo his wrinkled finger was hovering near. It was a passport photo, and in one corner you could see a quarter of a stamp and a quarter of a swastika. The photo was of a handsome young man in uniform with a slightly sullen look on his face. Apparently the old man himself. As I was looking at the picture, his wrinkled finger wandered over to indicate the next photo to the right.

"And that's Elsa. She was my sweetheart."

The picture showed a sharp-featured face, and at first glance I couldn't tell if it was a boy or a girl. But "Elsa" was wearing a different uniform from the soldier or Hitler Youth member next to her. So it might have been a girl.

He asked whether he should tell the story of his relationship with Elsa, and since he'd picked up the rifle again — without thinking, as if it was just an extension of his body or a part of his history — we could hardly say no. So we listened to his story.

It wasn't a proper story. At least it wasn't told the way people normally tell a story about the love of their life.

"I was a communist," he said. "Elsa and I were communists. Devoted communists. And not just after 1945 like all the rest of them. We'd always been communists. That's how we met — in a resistance group named after Ernst Roehm. Nobody would believe it all now, but that was a different time. And I had no equal when it came to marksmanship. Elsa was the only girl in the group, very reputable, from a good family, and she looked like a boy. She had translated lots of forbidden literature. She had translated that Jew Shakespeare. She'd translated Ravage. She could speak English exceptionally well, and not many people could back then. And I typed it up for her on a typewriter — yeah, that's how it was back then. Love of my life, fire of my loins. In the concentration camp they gassed Elsa right away. I was conscripted into a penal battalion and sent with my rifle to the Battle of Kursk. I could pick off an Ivan from four hundred meters."

"A what?" asked Tschick.

"An Ivan. A goddamn Russian," said the old man, pausing to think. He didn't look at me or Tschick, and Tschick and I were able to exchange a quick glance. Tschick didn't seem particularly uneasy, and I wasn't anymore either.

"I thought . . ." I said. "Weren't the Russians also some kind of communists?"

"Yes."

He thought silently again. "And I could hit one in the eye from four hundred meters. Horst Fricke, the best sharpshooter in his unit. I had more oak leaf clusters on my chest than an entire damn forest. I picked them off like clay pigeons. They were crazy. Or rather, the commanders were crazy. They drove the hordes at us. Private Sinning cleaned things up at the front with a machine gun, and Fricke was the rear guard. Sometimes it was Fricke alone versus Ivan. And they were armed too. Think about that before you ask such stupid questions. Talking about morals and all that crap. It was me or them! That was the only question. More Ivans every day, youthful flesh tumbling toward us. An ocean of flesh. They had a lot of it. All that living space out east. There were just too many Russians. And behind every line the Cheka, the counterrevolutionary police, shooting anyone who wouldn't run into our barrage of fire. Everyone thinks the Nazis were so bad. But compared to the Russians? Pissants. And that's how they finally overran us. With flesh. They never would have managed it with machines. One Ivan and another Ivan and another Ivan. I had a callus on my trigger finger as big as a grape. Look."

He held up both of his pointer fingers. And sure enough, the one on his right hand had a bulge near the first knuckle. Of course, I had no way of knowing if it really came from shooting Ivan.

"This is all a bunch of crap," said Tschick.

Oddly enough, the man didn't really react to this. He kept talking for a while, though we never did find out what it all had to do with the love of his life.

"There's one thing you need to understand, my doves," he said, finishing up. "Everything is meaningless. Love too. Carpe diem."

Then he pulled a little brown glass bottle out of his pants pocket and handed it to us as if it was the most precious thing on Earth. He made a big fuss about it, but he didn't want to say what was in the bottle. The label was yellowed and the bottle looked as if it had been in his pocket since he fought in the Battle of Kursk. We should open it only in case of an emergency, he said, only if the situation was so dire that we no longer knew what to do. Not before that point. And this stuff would help us. Actually he said *save*. It would save our lives.

We took it with us and walked out to the car. I held the bottle up to the light but couldn't tell what it was. Some viscous liquid and something solid.

Once in the car, Tschick tried without luck to decipher what was left on the label. And when he finally opened it, the car started to reek of rotten eggs and he tossed it out the window.

The road petered out at the edge of town, and we had to go cross-country. The chasm we'd crossed was off to the left somewhere. A long gravel embankment fell away to the right. In between was a forty- or fifty-meter-wide berm — like a small plateau. I turned around and in the distance I saw the village, the two-story house where sharpshooter Fricke lived, and — that a police car was pulled up in front of the house. It was tiny from this distance, barely visible, but it was unmistakable — the cops. The car seemed to be turning. I pointed it out to Tschick and we took off across the dirt. The berm kept getting narrower and the cliff edge kept getting closer. Then we saw the autobahn running below as it snaked around the gravel embankment. I could see a little rest area with two picnic benches, a Dumpster, and an emergency call box. We could probably drive straight onto the autobahn there — if we could find a way down. We were at the end of the damn plateau. I looked frantically out the back window as Tschick aimed the car at the embankment, a forty-five-degree slope covered with gravel and boulders.

"Down?" he yelled. I didn't know how to answer. He hit the brakes one last time, and then we were over the brink and that was it — we were hurtling down the embankment.

We probably could have made it if we had driven straight down. But Tschick tried to go sideways and switch back and there was no stopping the Lada at that point. We started skidding, got hung up on something, and flipped over. We rolled over three, four, five, six — I don't know how many times — and came to rest upside down. I wasn't sure what had happened. What I was sure of, though, was that the passenger door was open, so I tried to climb out. But I couldn't. It took about half an hour before I realized the reason I couldn't get out wasn't because I was injured but because I hadn't unbuckled my seat belt. Then I was finally out and I noticed the following things: a green Dumpster directly in front of me, an overturned Lada with steam coming out of the hood and hissing, and Tschick crawling along the ground on all fours. He hoisted himself up, stumbled for a few steps, and yelled, "Come on!" and started to run.

I didn't run. Where were we going to run? Behind us was the plateau and most likely the cops, in front of us was the autobahn, and beyond the autobahn were fields stretching to the horizon. Not exactly the ideal topography to escape from the law. There were a few trees and bushes around the rest area, and off across the fields was a big white box — probably a factory.

"What's going on?" Tschick yelled. "Are you hurt?"

Was I hurt? No, apparently not. Maybe a few bruises.

"Is something wrong?" he asked, coming back toward me.

I wanted to offer an explanation for why I thought it was such a stupid idea to try to escape on foot. Then there was a rustling of leaves and cracking of branches, and a hippo came through the bushes in front of us. Somewhere in Germany, right on the side of the autobahn, in the middle of a wasteland, a hippo came out of the bushes and rushed at us. It was wearing a blue pantsuit, had a curly blond perm, and was carrying a fire extinguisher in its hand. Four or five rings of fat jiggled around its waist. It had two barrels sticking out of the bottom of the pantsuit, and it stomped across the ground, stopped in front of the overturned Lada, and held up the fire extinguisher.

Nothing was burning.

I looked at Tschick and Tschick looked at me. We looked at the woman. Because that's what it was. A woman, not a hippo. Nobody said a word and I was thinking that a jet of white would shoot out of the fire extinguisher and bury us beneath a mountain of foam.

The woman waited a while for the car to explode in flames so she could put her fire extinguisher to use. But the Lada was just as underwhelming in death as it had been in life. There was only a hissing from the engine compartment. One of the back wheels was still spinning, getting slower and slower, and then it stopped.

"Are you boys okay?" the woman asked, still looking warily at the hood of the car.

Tschick tapped his finger on the fire extinguisher. "Something burning?" he said.

"Oh my God," the woman said lowering the extinguisher. "Did anything happen to you?"

"Nothing," said Tschick.

"You're not hurt?"

I shook my head.

"Where is your father? Or your mother? Who was driving?"

"I was driving," said Tschick.

"You just got the car from . . ."

"It's stolen," said Tschick.

If the doctor who later examined me was right, I was in shock during this time. When you're in shock all the blood rushes to your legs and there's basically no more blood in your head and you can't think straight. At least, that's what the doctor said. He also said it was a reaction from caveman times — when the Neanderthals were wandering through the woods and a mammoth suddenly appeared, they went into shock, and all the blood in their legs allowed them to run away faster. Thinking wasn't so important back then. Sounds odd to me, but that's what the doctor told me. Maybe Tschick had been right to try to run away and maybe I was stupid not to, but hindsight is twenty-twenty. And here was a woman standing in front of us with a fire extinguisher — and she was shocked too. Because even though I was in shock, and Tschick was in shock, this woman was in much worse shape. It would have been enough just to see the car flip down the hill or to have Tschick tell her it was a stolen car. She was shaking really bad. She looked at Tschick, pointed to a trickle of blood running down his chin, and said, "Oh my God." Then the extinguisher fell from her hand and onto Tschick's foot. He immediately fell to the ground, lifting his leg, grabbing it with his hands, and screaming.

"Oh my God!" the woman screamed again, kneeling next to Tschick in the grass.

"Shit," I said. I took a quick look at the ridge above us — still no cops.

"Is it broken?"

"How should I know?" screamed Tschick, rolling around in pain.

CHAPTER THIRTY EIGHT

So this was the situation: We'd driven hundreds of miles around Germany, ridden over an abyss on a scaffold, been shot at by Horst Fricke, had gone off the end of an embankment and rolled the car a half-dozen times, and come through it all basically unscathed — and then a hippo charged out of the bushes and destroyed Tschick's foot with a fire extinguisher.

We leaned down over his foot but had no idea if it was broken or just bruised. One thing was clear — Tschick couldn't stand on it.

"I'm so sorry!" said the woman. And she really did feel bad, you could tell. She seemed more pained than Tschick, at least judging by their faces. But while my head was still reeling and Tschick was rolling around on the ground moaning, she was the first one to get herself together. She felt Tschick's chin again and then lifted his lower leg in the air. "Ouch," she said as she twisted his ankle this way and that, and Tschick whimpered.

"You need to go to the hospital" was her conclusion.

"Hang on," I wanted to say, but the hippo had already shoved her front hooves under Tschick and lifted him up as easily as if he were a piece of toast.

Tschick screamed, but more out of surprise than pain. She disappeared through the bushes as quickly as she had come. I ran after them.

Beyond the shrubs was a green BMW 5 Series. The woman tossed Tschick into the passenger seat. I got in the back. When she climbed into the driver's seat, the car sunk two feet on her side and Tschick bounced up in his seat. Crazy, I thought, but it turned out I should have saved that word for what happened during the next few minutes.

"We have to hurry!" said the woman gravely, though when she said it presumably she wasn't thinking about fleeing from the police.

I was the only one who kept turning around and noticed that the police car must have managed to find a way down the embankment — because in the far distance the car was fighting its way through the scrub brush at the base of the slope.

"Buckle up," said the woman, stepping on the gas pedal. The BMW was doing a hundred kilometers an hour in two seconds. As she went around bends, I was thrown around the backseat like a paper airplane. Tschick was moaning.

"Put your seat belt on," she repeated.

I clicked my seat belt.

"What about you?" said Tschick to the woman.

Through the back window, I could see the traffic behind us recede. Somewhere in the distance you could hear a police siren, but not for long. And no wonder — we were up to two hundred and fifty kilometers an hour. Neither the woman nor Tschick seemed to have heard the siren. They were still talking about seat belts.

"It's not my car," said the woman. "I need a belt two meters long." She giggled. She spoke in a normal voice, but when she giggled it was squeaky, like the sound a little girl would make while being tickled.

When we came upon any obstacles, the woman honked her horn or flashed her lights. And if that didn't work she just calmly blew past them in the service lane as if she was pulling through the McDonald's drive-in. She'd obviously gotten over her shock.

"It's permitted in an emergency," she said. Then she giggled again. "So you guys were driving that car?"

"We're on vacation," said Tschick.

"And you stole it?"

"Borrowed, actually," said Tschick. "Or stolen. But we were going to take it back. I swear."

The BMW barreled along. The woman didn't respond. What could she have said? We had stolen a car and she had dropped a fire extinguisher on Tschick's foot. Studying her in the rearview mirror, I couldn't tell what kind of look flashed across her face, if any look flashed across her face at all. She certainly didn't seem hysterical.

She passed two tractor-trailers, and then she said, "So you guys are car thieves."

"If you say so," said Tschick.

"I say so."

"What are you?"

"This car belongs to my husband."

"No, I mean, what do you do for a living? And do you know where there's a hospital?"

"The hospital's not far from here. And I'm a speech therapist."

"What does a speech therapist do therapy on?" asked Tschick. "People's language?"

"I teach people to speak."

"Babies or what?"

"No. Children sometimes. But mainly adults."

"You teach adults to talk? Illiterate people or something?" Tschick grimaced, totally focused on the woman. I think he was basically trying to keep his mind off the pain in his foot, but the topic of conversation really did seem to grab him.

As the two of them were talking up front, I spent the whole time looking out the back. I probably missed some parts of the conversation. And like I said, I was in shock. But what I caught was the following:

"Vocal formation," said the woman. "Singers, people who do a lot of public speaking, people who mumble. Most people don't speak properly. You don't speak properly, actually."

"But you can still understand me."

"It's about your voice. You need to project your voice, it needs to resonate. See, your voice comes from here," she said, indicating her throat. Probably without even noticing it, she had let up on the gas a little once they had started talking. We were only going about a hundred and eighty now. I tapped Tschick on the shoulder, but he was deep into the conversation.

"I talk with my mouth."

"Normal speech has nothing to do with being able to project your voice. A good, resonant voice comes from here, from the core. But when you talk it comes from here. It needs to come from here." As she said the last "here," she hit herself twice beneath her breasts, making a sound something like *hee-R-R*.

"From hee-R-R?" said Tschick, hitting himself on the chest the same way.

"You have to think of it like athletics. The whole body is involved. The diaphragm, the abdominal muscles, the pelvis, it takes all of them. Two-thirds comes from the diaphragm versus only one third from the lungs."

Now we were down to a hundred and sixty kilometers an hour. If this kept up, she'd bring the car to a halt with her speech therapy.

"The important thing is to get to the hospital quickly," I said.

"It's okay," said Tschick. "It doesn't hurt so bad anymore."

I buried my head in my hands.

"When you talk from here," said the woman, "you get nothing but a little croaking sound. The air comes out of your throat — *uh, uh*. It has to come from here." She opened her mouth into a big O, held her hands in front of her gut, and lifted them as though she were hoisting an invisible box. She had to let go of the steering wheel to do it. Tschick reached across and steadied the wheel.

"From here," said the woman, calling, "Oooo!"

It scared me. But Tschick was all excited. I tried again to gesture to him, but he didn't understand it. Or he wasn't paying attention. Or maybe the woman's state of mind had infected him. The speedometer said one hundred and forty kilometers an hour. Still no sign of the cops.

"Oooo! Oooo! Oooo!" went the woman.

"Uh! Uh!" went Tschick.

"More in the middle, and move it down," said the woman, stepping on the gas again. "The human body is like a tube of toothpaste — when you squeeze it, something comes out the top. Oooooo! Ooooo!"

"Uh! Uh!" went Tschick.

"Better. Ooooooaaaaaaaah!"

"Ooaaah!"

That's seriously how it went — all the way to the hospital.

We catapulted down the off-ramp, made two hard rights, and two minutes later we pulled up in front of a huge white building in the middle of nowhere. No cops in sight.

"An excellent hospital," said the woman.

"I don't have any health insurance," said Tschick.

The woman looked briefly upset. Then she leaned across Tschick and opened the door for him. "Don't worry. I'm the one who hurt you, and I'll pay for it, of course. Or my insurance will. Or whatever. Keep your chin up."

There was a lot of activity in the emergency room. It was Sunday night, and there were at least twenty people waiting around. At the check-in desk, a man wearing stone-washed jeans was puking into a bucket he was holding under one arm while holding out his insurance card with the other arm.

"Please wait outside," a nurse said to us.

Tschick and I sat down on two free plastic chairs. After we'd been waiting for a while, the speech therapist went to the vending machines to buy drinks and candy bars. While she was away, we were called. Tschick couldn't stand on his foot, so I went up to the desk to explain the situation.

"And what is his name?"

"André." I said it the French way. "André Langin."

"Address?"

"Fifteen Wald Street, Berlin."

"Insurance?"

"DDK."

"You mean DBK?"

"Yep, that's it." DBK. I'd heard André bragging about it during his physical on health day. How great it was to have such top-notch health coverage. What an asshole. Though of course now I was happy about it too. My voice was cracking a little. Guess I should have done a bit of speech therapy in the car too.

I was mostly nervous about what all they would ask me next. I'd never been to an emergency room before.

"Birth date?"

"Thirteenth of July, 1996." I had no idea when André's birthday was. I was just hoping they wouldn't be able to check it too quickly.

"And what's wrong with him?"

"A fire extinguisher fell on his foot. And he might have hit his head too. It's bleeding. The woman there" — I pointed to the speech therapist, who was walking back toward Tschick with an armful of candy bars — "can confirm everything."

"Don't talk my ear off," said the nurse. She'd had her eye on the man with the bucket the entire time and seemed constantly on the verge of standing. In fact, during the minute I was standing there talking to her, she got out of her chair twice, like she was going to go over there and take away the bucket, but she sat back down both times.

"The doctor will call you."

The doctor will call us. It was that easy.

The speech therapist was somewhat surprised I'd taken care of the health insurance issue. She looked at me with her head cocked to the side.

"I just gave them my name," I said.

She sat with us, waiting for us to be called. We told her she didn't have to, but I think she felt guilty. For hours, she talked to us about speech therapy, video games, movies, girls, and car thieves. She was really nice. When we told her about trying to write our names in the wheat field with the Lada, she giggled the whole time. And when we told her we were probably going to take the train back home to Berlin when we got out of the hospital, she believed us.

They kept rushing people with blood streaming down them through the emergency room waiting area. And when it was almost midnight and they still hadn't called us, the woman finally said good-bye. She must have asked us a thousand times if there was anything else she could do for us. She gave us her address in case we needed it to get reimbursed for the medical bills, and gave us two hundred Euros to pay for the train tickets. I was a little embarrassed, but I wasn't sure how to turn it down. And then she said something weird when she was leaving. She looked at us, after having done everything anyone in her position could possibly do, and said, "You two look like potatoes." Then she walked away. She pushed her way through the revolving door and was gone. I found it unbelievably funny. To this day, I still laugh every time I think of it: You two look like potatoes. I don't know if anyone will understand it, but she really was the nicest of all.

Tschick finally got to see the doctor. A minute later he came back out. We had to go upstairs for an X-ray. I was getting more and more tired. At some point I dozed off on a bench in the hall, and when I woke up, Tschick was standing in front of me on crutches. His foot was in a cast. A real plaster cast, not some plastic splint.

A nurse put a few painkillers in his hand and told us we had to wait because the doctor needed to look at his foot again. I wondered who had put the cast on if it wasn't the doctor. The janitor? The nurse took us to an empty room where we could wait. There were two freshly made beds in the room.

The mood was no longer a happy one. Our trip was over. Even if nobody except us knew about it. We were pretty miserable. I had no desire to go anywhere on the train. Tschick's pills took a while to work. He lay in bed moaning. I went to the window and peered out. It was still dark out, but when I pressed my nose against the glass and put a hand on each side of my face, I could make out the coming dawn. I saw a hint of light and . . .

I told Tschick to turn off the light. He used one of his crutches as a remote control. The landscape became much more visible. I saw one lonely phone booth along the hospital driveway. I saw a sole concrete block. I saw a desolate fence, and a field. Some open land. Something about this area seemed familiar. As it got lighter, I could make out three vehicles on the other side of the strip. Two cars and a giant tow truck with a crane on it.

"You are not going to believe what I'm looking at."

"What is it?"

"I'm not sure."

"What is it?"

"Have a look."

"I'm not looking at shit," said Tschick. And then, after a pause, "What is it?"

"Seriously, you really have to see it for yourself."

He groaned. I heard him fiddle with the crutches. Then he pressed his face to the glass next to mine.

"It can't be," he said.

"I know," I said.

We stared out over the plowed field we had seen a few hours before from the other side. There'd been a white box on the horizon then. We were in that white box now. The speech therapist had driven in a big loop.

The sun had yet to break over the horizon, but you could already see the black Lada in the rest area next to the autobahn. It was upright now, resting on its wheels. They must have turned it back over. The trunk was open and three men were walking around the car, standing next to it, walking around it some more. One was in uniform, two in the overalls typical of sanitation workers. At least that's what it looked like from a distance. The crane on the tow truck was being maneuvered over the Lada, and somebody was putting chains around the wheels. The uniformed man closed the trunk, opened it again, then shut it again. Then he went over to the cab of the tow truck. Then two people went back over to the Lada. Then one went over to the truck again.

"What are they doing?" asked Tschick.

"Can't you see?"

"No, I mean, what are they *doing*?"

He was right. They were just walking back and forth doing this or that, doing the same things over and over again, but really doing nothing. Maybe they were looking for clues or something. We watched for a while longer, then Tschick lay back down in bed, moaning, and said, "Wake me up if anything happens."

But nothing happened. One of the men tested the chains, one went back over to the tow truck, one smoked.

Suddenly the view disappeared because the light went on in our room. The doctor was standing in the doorway, breathing loudly. In one of his nostrils was a blood-soaked cotton ball hanging down to his upper lip. He slowly shuffled over to Tschick's bed.

"Lift up your leg," he said. He had a voice like a war-movie general.

Tschick hoisted the cast. With one hand the doctor jiggled the cast, while with the other he held the wadding in his nose. He grabbed an X-ray out of a folder and held it up to the light. Then he threw it onto the bed next to Tschick and shuffled back out. He turned around in the doorway and said, "Contusion, hairline fracture, fourteen days." Then he rolled his eyes. Then, like he was steadying himself, he leaned against the door frame. He took a deep breath and said, "It's no big deal. Fourteen days off your foot. Consult your own doctor once you're home." He looked at Tschick, gauging whether he'd understood him, and Tschick nodded.

The doctor closed the door behind him as he left. But two seconds later he threw it open again, now seemingly wide awake. "A joke!" he said, smiling first at Tschick, then at me. "What's the difference between a doctor and an architect?"

We didn't know. So he gave the answer. "A doctor buries his mistakes."

"Huh?" said Tschick.

The doctor swatted the air with his hand. "If you get tired, there's coffee in the nurse's station. You can help yourselves. Good ol' caffeine."

He closed the door again. I had no time to wonder why the doctor was so weird because I went straight to the window. Tschick shut off the light with one of his crutches, and I just caught sight of the police driving off on the autobahn. The tow truck was already gone. The Lada was all by itself in the parking lot of the rest area. Tschick didn't believe me.

"Did the tow truck break down or something?"

"No clue."

"Well, it's now or never."

"What?"

"What do you mean, *what*?" He hit a crutch against the window.

"There's no way it'll still drive," I said.

"Why not? And if it won't, who cares. We at least need to get our stuff out of it. Even if it can't be driven . . ."

"There's no way you can still drive it."

"Still drive what?" asked a nurse, switching on the light. She had Tschick's — or rather André's — file in one hand and two cups of coffee on a tray in the other.

"Your name is André Langin," I whispered while rubbing my eyes like I was blinded by the light. Tschick said something about how we needed to get home. And unfortunately, that was exactly the reason the nurse wanted to talk to us.

Berlin was pretty far away, she said — where were we headed now? I told her we were staying in the area with an aunt and that it was all no problem. I shouldn't have said that. The nurse didn't ask where the aunt lived, but she took me to the nurse's station and put a phone in my hand. Tschick suppressed his pain, staggered out on his crutches, and said that we could go by foot. The nurse said, "Go ahead and try her first. Or don't you know the number?"

"Of course I do," I said. I saw a phone book on the table and didn't want that shoved into my hands next. So I dialed a random number hoping nobody would answer. Four in the morning.

I heard it ring. The nurse probably heard it too, since she was standing right there next to us. The smart thing would have been to call my own house, because it was a sure bet that nobody would answer there. But to do that I would have had to dial the Berlin area code first, and the nurse already looked suspicious enough as it was. It rang once, twice, three times, four. I was getting ready to hang up and say our aunt must still be asleep and that we could just walk . . .

"Errm, uh, Reiber residence," said a man's voice.

"Oh, hi, Aunt Mona!"

"This is the Reiber residence," said the man sleepily. "No aunt. No Mona."

"Did I wake you?" I asked. "Of course, stupid question. Here's the deal." I gestured to the nurse that everything was taken care of so she could get back to work if she needed to.

Apparently there was no work to be done, because she stayed as still as a statue.

"You must have the wrong number," I heard the voice say. "This is Mr. Reiber."

"Yeah, I know. I hope you didn't . . . yeah, oh yes," I said, signaling to Tschick and the nurse how surprised and worried Aunt Mona was to get a call from us at this hour.

The silence on the line now was almost as annoying as the throat-clearing and coughing had been.

"Yeah, no, well, something happened," I continued. "André had a little accident. Something fell on his foot. No, no. We're at the hospital. They put a cast on him."

I looked at the nurse. She still didn't budge.

There were some unintelligible noises from the other end of the line, and then the voice was there again. He didn't sound so sleepy anymore. "I get it," said the man. "We're having a pretend conversation."

"Yes," I said. "But it's no big deal. It's not too serious — just a hairline fracture or whatever."

"And I am Aunt Mona."

"No — I mean, yes, yes, exactly."

"There's somebody next to you, listening." The man made a noise of some sort. I wasn't sure, but I thought he might be quietly laughing.

"Yep, yeah . . ."

"And if I shout really loud right now, you'd have a major problem on your hands, right?"

"Please, no, uh . . . no. You really don't need to worry. Everything's all taken care of."

"It's not taken care of," said the nurse. "She needs to pick you up."

"Do you need help?" asked the man.

"What?"

The nurse looked as if she was going to grab the phone from me any second to speak to Aunt Mona herself.

"You have to pick us up, Aunt Mona. Can you? Yes?"

"I don't really understand what this is about," said the man on the phone, "but it sounds like you're in real trouble. Is someone threatening you?"

"No."

"I mean, a broken ankle, making a fake call at four in the morning, and you sound like you can't be a day over thirteen. You must be in trouble."

"Well, yeah."

"And obviously you can't say what it is. So one more time: Do you need help?"

"No."

"Are you sure? This is the last time I'm going to offer."

"No."

"Okay, I'll just listen, then," said the man.

"In any event, if you could maybe pick us up in the car," I said, sounding embarrassed.

"Not if you don't want me to," the man said, chuckling. And that threw me off. If he had hung up or yelled at me, I would have understood that at four in the morning. But the fact that he was amused and offered to help us, that was crazy. Ever since I was a little boy my father had told me that the world was a bad place. The world is bad and people are bad. Don't trust anyone, don't talk to strangers, all of that. My parents drilled that into me, my teachers drilled that into me, even TV drilled that into me. When you watched the local news — people were bad. When you saw primetime investigative shows — people were bad. And maybe it was true, maybe ninety-nine percent of people were bad. But the strange thing was that on this trip, Tschick and I had run into almost only people from the one percent who weren't bad. And now here I was, getting a random stranger out of bed at four A.M., for no good reason, and he was super nice and even willing to help us. Maybe they should tell you about things like that in school too, just so you're not totally surprised by it. I was so surprised that all I could do was kind of stutter.

"Yeah, twenty minutes, great, yeah. You'll pick us up. Good." For the grand finale of my performance, I turned to the nurse and asked, "What's the name of this hospital again?"

"Wrong question!" hissed the man immediately.

The nurse furrowed her brow. My God, was I an idiot.

"Virchow Hospital," she said slowly. "It's the only one within *fifty* kilometers."

"Exactly," said the man.

"Ah, she just said the same thing," I said, pointing to the phone.

"So you're also not from around here," said the man. "You must have really gotten yourselves into some shit. I hope I can read about it in the paper tomorrow."

"Yeah, me too," I said. "Definitely. We'll be waiting."

"Okay, good luck," said the man.

"Thanks!"

The man laughed again and hung up.

"Was she *laughing*?" said the nurse.

"This isn't the first time we've made her worry," said Tschick, who had only gotten half of the conversation. "She's been through this before."

"And she thinks it's funny?"

"She's *cool*," said Tschick, emphasizing the word "cool" in a way that said not everyone in the room was cool.

We stood by the phone for a few minutes; then the nurse said, "You're a couple of rascals."

Then she let us leave.

We sat down in front of the hospital entrance and acted as if we were keeping an eye out for Aunt Mona. Once we were sure nobody was watching us anymore, we took off. I ran and Tschick hobbled. There was a fence at the edge of the field. Tschick threw his crutches over and then threw himself over. A few yards into the field he got stuck. The field was freshly plowed and the crutches sank into the dirt like a hot knife in butter. It wasn't going to work. He started swearing, left the crutches sticking up, and hopped along with one arm around my shoulders. When we had made it across about a third of the field, we turned around. The landscape was blue. Light from the sun, which was still hidden behind the hospital building, shone through the mist and the tops of trees. The crutches, still sticking up, though one had drooped to the side, looked like a cross. In one of the windows of the upper story of the hospital building — maybe even the same window we'd looked out and seen the Lada — there was a shape in white scrubs looking out at us. Probably the nurse thinking about what a couple of nut-jobs she'd just taken care of. If she had realized how crazy we really were, she probably wouldn't have been standing there, just watching.

But she must have seen where we were heading, and she probably also saw us arrive at the car. The roof and the passenger side were dinged up, but not so badly that you couldn't sit comfortably inside. The passenger door couldn't be opened, but you could slide across from the driver's side. The interior looked like a dump. The accident, being flipped over, and then being flipped back up, had sent everything flying all over the place — all our supplies, jam jars, gas canister, empty bottles, sleeping bags. The Richard Clayderman cassette was stuck between the seats. The hood of the car was slightly buckled, and the part of the roof where the car had been lying upside down was smeared with sand-covered oil. "That's it," I said.

Tschick squeezed himself into the driver's seat but couldn't get his plaster-covered foot onto the gas pedal — the cast was too wide. He put the car in neutral, squirmed in the seat a little, and tapped the gas with his left foot. The engine fired right up. Tschick shifted into the passenger seat. I said, "You must have lost your mind."

"All you have to do is push the gas and steer," he said. "I'll shift."

I sat down at the wheel and told Tschick it wasn't going to work. There was half a tank of gas, and the motor was idling smoothly, but when I looked at the autobahn and saw the cars going by at two hundred kilometers an hour, I knew it wasn't going to work.

"I have to tell you a secret," I said. "I'm the biggest coward in the world. The most boring person on the planet and the biggest coward. We'll have to walk. Maybe I could give it a try on a dirt track or something. But not on the autobahn."

"Why would you possibly say you were boring?" asked Tschick. So I asked him if he realized why I had even agreed to go with him to Wallachia in the first place. Namely, because I was boring — so boring, in fact, that I didn't get invited to a party that everyone else got invited to. So I had decided for once in my life *not* to be boring. Tschick said I was nuts and that he hadn't been bored for a single second since he had gotten to know me. That on the contrary this had been the coolest and most exciting week of his entire life. Then we talked about the coolest and most exciting week of our lives — and it was hard to accept that it was now over.

Tschick looked at me for a long time and said it wasn't true that Tatiana didn't invite me because I was boring, and it wasn't true that she didn't like me for that reason either.

"Girls don't like you because they're afraid of you. That's what I think. Because you don't pay them attention and because you're not a kiss-ass like André Langin. You're not boring, you idiot. Isa liked you right away. Because she's not as stupid as she looks. She actually has a brain — unlike Tatiana."

I looked at Tschick. I think my jaw must have been hanging open.

"Yeah, yeah, you're in love with Tatiana. And she's good looking, for sure. But seriously, compared to Isa she's a total moron. And I'm a good judge of that, unlike you. Because — can I tell you a secret?" Tschick gulped, and looked as if he had a cannonball stuck in his throat. He was silent for at least five minutes. Then he said he could judge them because he wasn't interested in them. Girls. Then he was silent again for a while. He had never told anyone, he said, and now he had told me, but I didn't need to worry about it. He wasn't looking for anything from me, he knew I was into girls and all that, but that he just wasn't that way and there was nothing he could do about it.

You can think what you want about me, but I wasn't that surprised. I really wasn't. I didn't know it for a fact, but I guess I had a feeling. Really. When he talked about his uncle in Moscow the very first time we were in the car, the whole thing about my jacket, the way he treated Isa. I mean, obviously I didn't know for sure. But in retrospect it seems as if I had some idea.

Tschick rested his head on the dashboard. I put a hand on his back. We sat there and listened to "Ballade pour Adeline," and I thought for a few minutes about what it would be like to be gay. It could really have been the solution to all my problems. But it wasn't going to work. I mean, I really liked Tschick, but I knew I liked girls. Then I put the Lada into first gear and started to move. It had been so sad sitting in the hospital all night thinking about the fact that the trip was over. And it was so fantastic to be looking out the windshield again with the steering wheel in my hand. I practiced a little in the parking lot. I was still having trouble shifting, but when Tschick took over that duty, leaving me just to push the clutch, it was okay. So we accelerated onto the on-ramp. Then I pulled into the emergency lane and stopped.

"Take it easy," said Tschick. "Easy does it. Let's try it again."

We waited for another gap in traffic. And by that I mean we waited until there wasn't another car in sight. Then I stepped on it again and accelerated.

"Shift!" shouted Tschick, and I stepped on the clutch pedal as he put it into second gear.

I was sweating like crazy.

"It's all clear, merge!" Tschick put it into third gear and then fourth, and I slowly relaxed.

I flinched again when the first fat Audi zoomed by doing five hundred kilometers an hour or whatever, but after a while I got used to it and realized driving on the autobahn was actually easier than on smaller roads where you're constantly braking and shifting and accelerating. Here I had a lane to myself and just had to go straight. I watched the lane markers racing toward me like in a video game — but it looked totally different in the driver's seat of a real car. There's just no way to imitate it with PlayStation graphics. Sweat was still streaming down me, and my back clung to the seat. Tschick stuck a piece of black duct tape on my upper lip, and then we drove and drove.

Clayderman tinkled the ivories, and between him tinkling, the partially collapsed roof of the car, Tschick's messed-up foot, and the fact that we were doing a hundred in a rolling Dumpster, I was overcome with a strange feeling. It was a feeling of bliss, a feeling of invincibility. No accident, no authority, no law of nature could stop us. We were on the road and we would always be on the road. And we sang along to the music, at least as best as you can sing along to tinkling instrumental music.

We drove until it started to get dark, then turned off the auto-bahn onto a country road somewhere deep in the middle of nowhere. I drove in third gear, winding along between the fields. Everything was quiet. The evening was quiet and the fields were yellow and green and brown, and the color was seeping from the landscape as the light faded. Tschick had his arm out the window and his head on his arm. I had my arm out the window too, the way you do in a boat when you dip your fingers in the water. I felt tree leaves and plant stalks graze my hand as my other hand guided the Lada through the darkened landscape.

The last beams of light disappeared from the horizon. It was a moonless night, and I remembered the first time I saw what nighttime looked like, or at least the first time I realized what nighttime was. I was eight or nine and I have Herr Klever to thank. He lived in the apartment block across the street. We lived in an apartment block too, and at the end of the street was a big field of barley. I used to play with a girl named Maria in that barley field in the evening. We would crawl through the grain on all fours, making paths, creating a giant maze. And one night Herr Klever, an old man, showed up with his wiener dog and a flashlight. He lived on the third floor and was always shouting at us. He hated kids. He trudged around with his dog, shining his flashlight into the field and shouting that we were ruining the crops. He shouted that we had to come out immediately and that he was going to call the police and have us arrested and that we would have to pay a thousand Euro fine. We were eight or nine, like I said, and didn't know this was just the typical stupid crap old people say. In a panic we ran out of the field. Maria was smart and ran toward our apartment block. But I went the other way first, and the old man was there with his dog blocking the way. He stood his ground, fiddled with his flashlight, and kept shouting. So I ran in the opposite direction, back into the field.

I ran through the field and into Hogenkamp Road because I thought I might be able to go all the way back around. I knew the way from having done it during the day. But now the Hogenkamp was dark and seemed to be hemmed in by scrub brush. Just beyond was Hogenkamp playground — we never went there because there were older kids there. But at night, of course, it was empty. The giant zip line wasn't being used. It was a funny feeling. I could have had the whole place to myself, could have done whatever I wanted, but I didn't stop — I just kept running and running. There wasn't a single person anywhere around. Lights were on in front of little houses, and I kept running down another street, where there was also not a soul. It was a huge detour, making an arc out around the field of several miles. But back then I could run like a champ. And after a while I actually liked it — running through this dark, empty world. I wasn't even sure if I was still scared, and I stopped thinking about Herr Klever.

Obviously I'd been out at night other times, earlier in my

life. But it hadn't been the same. That had always been with my parents or in a car on the way home from a relative's house or whatever. This was a whole new world, a completely different world than it was during the day. It felt as if I'd just discovered America. I didn't see a single person the entire way. Then suddenly I saw two women. They were sitting on the steps in front of a Chinese restaurant, and I couldn't figure out what they were doing there. One of them was crying and shouting, "I'm not going in there! I'm not going in there again!" The other one was trying to calm her down, but to no effect. Above them, Chinese characters in yellow and red lit up the night. There were dark trees around the building. And in the foreground, an eight-year-old was jogging past. I was annoyed. The women were probably annoyed too, and also wondering what the heck an eight-year-old was doing out running at night. We looked at each other, them crying and me running. I have no idea why that made such a strong impression on me. I guess I'd never seen grown women crying before, and I thought about it a lot afterward. Anyway, this was a night like that.

I leaned my head to the side and looked out the window as the Lada quietly took the curves of the road through the blue-green grain fields of summer. At some point I said I wanted to stop, and I stopped. The countryside was dark, and we stood and looked out over a field where in the distance you could see the black shape of a farm. I was about to say something when off to our left a light went on in the window of another farmhouse. I didn't say anything after all. Then Tschick put his arm around my shoulders and said, "We've got to get going."

We got back in the car and drove on.

The next day we were back on the autobahn. A huge tractor-trailer passed us. It looked as if it was made out of pig stalls. A couple of wheels, a rusty cab, and license plates from Albania or something. It was only with a second glance that I saw that what looked like pig stalls actually were pig stalls. The cages were stacked next to each other and on top of each other, and out of every one peeked a pig.

"What a shit life," said Tschick.

The road slanted slightly uphill in this section, and it took the truck ages to pass us. When we could finally see its rear wheels, it started to drop back again. After a minute, the cab reappeared next to us. Somebody rolled down the window of the passenger door.

"Did he see you?" asked Tschick. "Or is he looking at the dents on our roof?"

I let up on the gas pedal to make it easier for him to get by us. The truck put its blinker on, swerved into our lane, and then started going slower.

"What the hell kind of idiot is this guy?" said Tschick.

We slowed way down.

"Pass him."

213

I went into the left lane. The truck swerved back into the left lane in front of us.

"Pass him on the right, then."

I steered back into the right lane. The truck got in the middle, straddling the two lanes, and to this day I don't know if he was trying to slow us down or if he was just a moron. Tschick said I should wait for another car to come along and then follow it past the truck. But no other cars came along. The autobahn was completely empty.

"Should I use the emergency lane?"

"Maybe if we can get a running start," said Tschick. "If you think you can do it. You'll have to shift."

We fell back, I stepped on the clutch, and Tschick put it in third. The engine whined.

"Now step on it — it'll take off like a rocket."

Rocket turned out not to be the best description. More like the shifting of a sand dune. We had fallen about a hundred and fifty or two hundred meters behind the truck, and even with the pedal to the metal it took about a minute before we got back up behind it. And the tachometer was quivering in the red by then. I pulled up right behind the truck so I'd be invisible to the driver. He was swerving back and forth, and I wasn't sure which side to pass him on.

"Swerve with him," said Tschick. "Then at the last second, zip by!"

I still had my foot all the way down on the gas pedal. I should point out that I wasn't nervous at that moment. I'd swerved like this a million times in video games. It came more naturally than driving straight. And the pig transporter was just the sort of obstacle you had to go around in driving games.

I pulled right up behind the truck so I could shoot around it in the emergency lane. And that's exactly what I would have done if Tschick hadn't been there. If Tschick hadn't been there, I wouldn't have survived.

"HIT THE BRAKES!" he screamed. "BRAAAAAKE!"

My foot stepped on the brake pedal even before I heard and understood his scream. My foot braked automatically because I was used to doing what he said to do when I was driving. So he shouted "brakes" and I braked — without knowing why. Because as far as I could tell there was no reason to brake.

There was space between the truck and the guardrail for at least five cars, and it would have been ages before I had realized that the truck hadn't made way but rather had *skidded* out of the way. The rear end of the trailer had slid sideways, and even though we were right behind the trailer I suddenly saw the cab directly in front of me in the middle of the road — and I saw the trailer overtaking the cab. The eighteen-wheeler was transforming itself into a barrier — and that barrier was skidding in front of us, across the entire width of the autobahn, as we skidded toward it. The scene was so strange that later I had the feeling it had taken several minutes to unfold. In reality, it didn't even last long enough for Tschick to scream "brake" a third time.

The Lada turned sideways. The barrier in front of us drifted backward, tipped over with a crash, and left us faced with eighteen rotating wheels. Thirty meters in front of us. In absolute silence we glided into those wheels, and I thought, *Okay, we're going to die.* I thought I would never get back to Berlin, I would never see Tatiana again, and I would never know whether she liked my drawing or not. I thought I needed to apologize to my parents and I thought, *Crap, I forgot to save the game.*

The other thing I thought was that I should tell Tschick that I'd nearly decided to become gay because of him. I was going to die sometime, so it might as well be now, I thought as we finally slid into the truck — and nothing happened. In my memory I didn't even hear a crash. Though there must have been an incredible crash. Because we rammed straight into the truck.

I didn't feel a thing for a minute. The first sensation I had was the feeling that I couldn't breathe. The seat belt was cutting me in half and my head was practically on the gas pedal. Tschick's cast was also somewhere near my head. I sat up. Or at least I turned my head. Above the cracked windshield was a truck tire obscuring the sky. It was turning silently. There was a dirty lightning bolt sticker on the hub of the wheel — a red bolt on a yellow background. A fist-sized clump of gunk dangled from the axle, slowly detached itself, and then splattered on the windshield.

"So much for that," said Tschick. He had survived.

Thunderous applause broke out. It sounded like a huge crowd was shouting, whistling, hooting, and stomping their feet, and it didn't seem completely unjustified — for an amateur driver, my braking performance had been top notch. At least that was my opinion, and it didn't surprise me that others thought so as well. It's just that there was actually no crowd there.

"Are you okay?" asked Tschick, shaking my arm.

"Yeah. You?"

The passenger side of the car next to Tschick had been crushed inward about a foot, but very evenly. There were shards of glass everywhere.

"I think I cut myself." He held up a bloody hand. The audience was still roaring and whistling, but those sounds were mixed with grunts now.

I extricated myself from the seat belt and fell onto my side. The car was apparently lying at an odd angle — I had to climb out the side window. I immediately fell over something in the street. I tried to get up but fell over again and landed in a pool of bloody sludge. A dead pig. A few yards behind us a red Opel had come to a stop. Inside the car were a man and a woman, both pushing down the door locks. I sat down on the hood of their car and grabbed the radio antenna. I wasn't able to stand anymore, and the antenna felt good in my hand. I never wanted to let go of it. For the rest of my life. "Are you okay?" Tschick called again when he had climbed out of the Lada.

At that moment, a screeching pig came running around the end of the overturned trailer. And then a bunch more. The lead pig ran, bleeding, across the autobahn and into some bushes. Some of the others ran after it, but most of them just stood there surrounded by dead pigs and battered stalls and screeched hysterically. Then I saw the police on the horizon. At first I wanted to run, but I knew there was no point. And the final two images that I can remember are of Tschick hobbling off into the bushes with his cast, and of the trooper standing next to me with a friendly look on his face, taking my hand off that antenna and saying, "It'll be okay without you."

I've already told you the rest.

"He doesn't understand."

My father turned to my mother and said, "He just doesn't understand. He's too stupid."

I was sitting on a chair and he was on another one facing me. He was bent over so far that his face was directly in front of mine and his knees were pressing against mine. I could smell his aftershave with every single word he shouted. Aramis. A gift from my mother for his hundred and seventieth birthday.

"You really screwed up. Is that clear?"

I didn't answer. What would I say? Of course it was clear. And he wasn't saying it for the first time. More like the hundredth time that day. I had no idea what he wanted to hear from me.

I looked at my mother. My mother coughed.

"I think he gets it," she said. She stirred her Amaretto with a straw.

My father grabbed me by the shoulders and shook me. "Do you understand what I'm saying? Kindly say something!"

"What do you want me to say? I've already said yes. Yes, I understand. Yes, it's clear."

"You don't understand a thing! Nothing is clear to you. He thinks this is just about saying the words. What an idiot!"

"I'm not an idiot just because for the hundredth time . . ."

Bam. He smacked my face.

"Josef, don't." My mother tried to stand up but lost her balance and let herself sink back into the armchair next to the bottle of Amaretto.

My father got right in my face. He was shaking with rage. Then he crossed his arms on his chest and I tried to put on a face creased with worry — because my father probably expected that, and because I knew his arms were only crossed because he was about to smack me again. Up to that point I had just said what I thought. I didn't want to lie. This face was the first lie that I trotted out — to speed things along.

"I know that we screwed up big-time, and I know . . ."

My father started to move his arms and I flinched. But this time he just yelled: "No, no, no! It's not *we* who screwed up, you idiot. It's your piece of trash Russian friend who screwed up. And you're so stupid that you let yourself get dragged into it. You're too stupid even to adjust a rearview mirror!"

My face showed my annoyance, because I'd already told him a thousand times what really happened — even if he didn't want to hear it.

"Do you think you're an island? Don't you realize this is going to fall on us? How do you think this makes me look? How can I sell somebody a house when my son might steal their car?"

"You aren't selling any houses anymore anyway. Your company is . . ."

Bam. The sound of his hand hitting my face made a crack. I fell to the floor. Moron. In school we were always told that violence is never the answer. My ass. When you get a smack in the face, you know damn well it's an answer.

My mother screamed, I got up, my father looked at my mother and then away again, and then he said, "Sure, sure, it doesn't matter anyway. Sit down. I said sit down, you idiot. You listen to me and you listen good. You've got a good chance of getting away with just a slap on the wrist. I know that from Schuback. Unless you act as idiotically as you are right now and you tell the judge how great you are at hotwiring cars with this and that wire and all that crap. They love doing that in the juvenile justice system — they bring charges against somebody so they will testify against others. And obviously that's what they plan to do to you too, except that you're too goddamn stupid. But you can be sure of one thing: Your Russian friend is not as stupid as you. He knows how it works. He's already got a criminal past — robbing stores with his brother, fraud, fencing stolen goods. Yeah, I see the look on your face. That's how those types of people operate. Of course he didn't tell you about it. He also doesn't have a nice home like this to show the court. He's living in a hole right now. In some closet-sized shit-hole. Where he belongs. He'll be lucky if he gets to stay in a juvenile detention center. Schuback says they could also deport him. And tomorrow he'll pay any price to save his own skin — do you understand? He already gave his statement and he put all the blame on you. It always works that way — every idiot tries to blame the others."

"And that's what I'm supposed to do too?"

"You're not just *supposed* to do it, you *will* do it. Because they'll believe you. Do you understand? Lucky for you the agent from Child Welfare was impressed with our place. How the house looked. You should have seen him looking at the pool. He said it straight out — that this was the right sort of house to raise a child in, with all the bells and whistles." My father turned to my mother and my mother stared into her glass. "You were dragged into it by that low-class Russian bastard. And that is exactly what you will tell the judge — regardless of what you told the police. Got it? Got it?"

"I'll tell the judge what happened," I said. "He's not stupid."

My father stared at me for approximately four seconds. That was the end. I saw a flash in his eyes; then I didn't see anything for a while. The blows struck me everywhere, and I fell off my chair and squirmed around on the floor with my forearms in front of my face. I heard my mother scream and fall over and shout "Josef!" By the end I was lying on the floor in such a way that between my arms I could see out the window to the backyard. I still felt the kicks, but they were coming more slowly. My back hurt. I saw the blue sky above the garden and sniffled. I saw the sides of the umbrella swaying in the wind above the lounge chair. Next to the chair was a brown man fishing leaves out of the pool with a dip net. They'd rehired the Indian.

"Oh, God, oh, God," said my mother, coughing.

I spent the rest of the day in bed. I lay on my side and toyed with the blinds, swinging in the afternoon sun above me. The blinds were ancient. I'd had them since I was three. We'd moved five times and still they'd always been there. That occurred to me for the first time as I played with them. I could hear my parents' voices outside in the backyard. Now they were giving an earful to the Indian. He must have missed a waterlogged leaf in the pool. It was my father's big day of yelling. Later I heard birds in the yard and the sun began to set. It got peaceful.

I lay there as it got darker and darker, stared at the blinds, and wondered how long things would be like this. How long could I lie here, how long we'd live in this house, how long my parents would still be married.

And I looked forward to seeing Tschick again. That was the only thing I looked forward to. I hadn't seen him since the accident on the autobahn, and that was four weeks ago now. I knew they'd taken him to a juvenile detention center. But it was a place where you weren't allowed to have any outside contact — you couldn't even get a letter.

CHAPTER
FORTY·SIX

Then came the court proceedings. I was dying from nervousness. The rooms alone were terrifying. Giant staircases, columns, statues on the wall like in a church. You also can't tell from watching courtroom TV shows that you have to wait around for hours and hours in a place that feels like a funeral home. I felt like I was waiting for my own funeral as I sat there. And I also thought to myself that I would never so much as steal a pack of gum again.

When I entered the courtroom, the judge was sitting behind his desk and pointed to the place I was supposed to sit down — at a table, kind of like at school. The judge was wearing a black poncho, and there was a woman sitting next to him who seemed to be surfing the Internet the whole time. At least that's what it looked like. She typed now and then, but she didn't look up from the computer for all the hours we were in the courtroom. Off to the left was another guy in a black poncho. That turned out to be the prosecutor. The black clothes were apparently an integral part of court cases. Out in the halls of the courthouse there were more people running around in black outfits, and the whole thing made me think of the white scrubs and lab coats of the hospital — and of nurse Hanna —

and I was glad at least that you couldn't see people's underwear through the black outfits.

Tschick wasn't there yet, but he came in about a minute later, escorted by someone from the juvenile detention center. We hugged each other and nobody tried to stop us. But we didn't have much time to chat. The judge got started right away. I had to say my name and address and all that, and then Tschick had to do the same. Then the judge basically repeated all the questions the police had already asked us. Not sure why, since he already knew our answers from the court documents. And as far as the facts of the case, there was no dispute. I told more or less the truth, the same as I did when the police asked me the questions. I mean, I left out a few tiny details — like the fact that we had used André Langin's name at the hospital. But that kind of stuff was okay to sweep under the rug — nobody cared about it. The main thing the judge wanted to know was *when* we first took the car, *where* we went with it, and *why* we did it. That last part was the only difficult question: Why? The police had kept asking us the same question, and now the judge, too, wanted to know. But I didn't know how to answer. Luckily he offered us potential answers — were we just trying to have fun? Fun. Well, yeah, fun, that seemed to me the most probable explanation even if I wouldn't have put it exactly that way. I couldn't really say what I was hoping to find in Wallachia. I had no idea. And I wasn't sure whether the judge would be interested in the whole Tatiana Cosic story. That I'd made a drawing for her and that I was afraid I might be the most boring person on Earth, and that for once in my life I didn't want to act like a coward. So I just said that his fun theory was right.

It also occurs to me that I lied about something else. It had to do with the speech therapist. I didn't want her to get into any trouble because of us, since she'd been so incredibly nice. So I just never mentioned her and the fire extinguisher. I said the same thing I'd told the police — that Tschick had broken his foot when the Lada flipped over coming down the embankment next to the autobahn, and that we had walked across the field to the hospital. Not a word about the speech therapist.

An okay lie, really. But even when I said it to the cops, it occurred to me that I'd probably get caught for it. Because Tschick would probably make up some other explanation when they asked him. And they would ask him. But oddly enough, the truth never came out because Tschick had exactly the same thought I did — he didn't want to drag the speech therapist into it either. And as it emerged in court that day, he had used the same explanation I had — that he'd broken his foot when the car went over the embankment and we'd limped through the field to the hospital. It never occurred to anybody that our story defied logic. Because when you end up in the middle of nowhere, in a place you've never been before, and you get into an accident, and all you can see are fields all around you and, in the distance, a white building with a couple of trees in front of it, how in the world would you know it was a hospital?

Anyway, like I said, the judge was more interested in other things.

"What I'd like to know is which of you initially had the idea to take this trip?" He addressed the question to me.

"The Russian of course!" came a voice from the gallery. My father, the idiot.

"The question is addressed to the accused," said the judge. "If I wanted your opinion, I would ask you."

"*We* had the idea," I said. "Both of us."

"No way," piped Tschick.

"We just wanted to drive around a little," I said. "Take a vacation, like normal people . . ."

"Not true," Tschick interjected.

"It's not your turn," said the judge. "Wait until I get to you."

The judge was strict. The only person allowed to speak was the one he spoke to. And when he got to Tschick, Tschick immediately said that it was his idea to go to Wallachia and that he'd had to practically drag me into the car. He explained that he knew how to drive and how to hotwire cars, and that I was so clueless I didn't know the gas pedal from the brake. He was talking complete nonsense, and I told the judge it was nonsense. And the judge said it wasn't my turn anymore, and I could hear my father groaning in the background.

After we had talked for long enough about the car, we came to the worst part — people talking *about* us. The man from the juvenile detention center testified about Tschick's background, talking about him as if he wasn't even there, basically saying his family was nothing more than trash — even if he didn't use that word. Then the guy from Child Welfare talked about his visit to my house, about what a filthy rich family I came from, how I was left unsupervised and neglected, and in the end he characterized my family as a kind of trash too. And when the verdict was read, I was surprised I wasn't given life in prison. Tschick had to stay in the detention center where he was already being held. And as for me, I was issued a directive to do community service. Seriously, that's what the judge said. Fortunately he explained what that meant — and in this case it meant I had to spend thirty hours wiping old people's asses. And then the whole thing finished up with an interminable lecture on morality, though what he said was actually okay. Not the kind of stuff my father says, or what you hear in school — it was more stuff that made you see things in terms of life and death, and I actually found myself listening closely to the judge because he didn't seem like a complete moron. On the contrary. He seemed pretty sensible. And his name was Burgmuller in case anyone is interested.

So that was the summer. And then it was time for school to start again. Instead of 8C, 9C was now posted on the door of the classroom. Nothing else had changed. Same seating chart. Everyone in the same spots as the previous year, except in the back row, where there was an empty seat. No Tschick.

First class on the first day of school: Mr. Wagenbach. I was a minute late, but for some reason I didn't get chewed out. I was still limping a little, and still had a few cuts on my face here and there. Wagenbach lifted one eyebrow and wrote the word "Bismarck" on the blackboard.

"Your classmate Tschichatschow will not be in class today," he said as an aside, but either he didn't know the reason for his absence or he didn't say. I don't think he knew the reason.

I was a little sad when I saw the empty seat, and sadder still when I glanced over at Tatiana, who was sitting there all tan, with a pencil in her mouth. She was listening to Wagenbach, and it was impossible to say if she was the proud owner of a pencil sketch of Beyoncé or if she had just crumpled it up and tossed it in the garbage. She looked so hot that morning that I had difficulty not constantly looking over at her. But with an iron will I kept myself from doing that.

I was trying to muster a little interest in Bismarck when Hans put a note on my thigh. I held it in my fist for a minute because Wagenbach was looking in my direction. Then I looked at it to see who I needed to pass it on to. But it said Mike. I couldn't remember getting a single note the previous school year. Except for the kind that everyone got — the ones that said stuff like *Don't look up, there are footprints on the ceiling* or other elementary school crap like that.

I waited another minute and then unfolded it and read. I read it five times straight. It wasn't such a complicated note — in fact, there were just ten words — but I still had to read it five times to understand it. It said: *My God, what in the world happened to you?!? Tatiana.*

I just couldn't get the last word through my head. I didn't look around.

The chance that somebody was trying to make an ass of me was relatively high. It was a common trick in the past — to send a fake note saying something like *I love you* or whatever. But you could usually tell who had really sent it because the person was trying to secretly watch you.

I looked in the direction the note had come from — which was also where Tatiana sat. Nobody seemed to be watching me. I read the note a sixth time. It was Tatiana's handwriting. I knew it well. The *A* with the rounded top, the curlicue of the *G*. I could imitate it perfectly. And of course if I could, so could everyone else. But just suppose — suppose — that it really was from her? Suppose the girl who didn't invite me to her party really wanted to know what had happened to me?

Wow. How should I answer? Assuming I did answer, that is. Because, after all, a lot had happened, and it would take hundreds of pages to explain it all. Though I would love to have done just that — written hundreds of pages. How we'd driven around, how we'd flipped the car, how Horst Fricke had shot at us. The moonscape we discovered, the whole debacle with the pigs, and a thousand other things. And how I'd dreamed that Tatiana was seeing it all. But I was pretty sure she didn't really want to know all the details. That the note was more out of politeness. I thought for a little while longer, and then I gathered myself and wrote, *Ah, nothing special*, and sent the note back.

I didn't look at Tatiana as she read it, but thirty seconds later it was back. This time there were only nine words. *Come on, tell me! I really want to know.*

She really wanted to know. I needed an eternity for my response. Despite the fact that again it wasn't very detailed. Of course, I secretly wanted to write my novel-length version for her. But there's not too much space on a piece of scrap paper. I put a lot of thought into it. Class was almost over when I wrote Tatiana's name on the outside again and handed it back to Hans. Hans passed it to Jasmin. Jasmin let it sit next to her for a while like she didn't care about it. Then she flipped it to Anja. Anja tossed it across the aisle onto Olaf's desk, and Olaf, who was as dumb as a box of rocks, was handing the note over André's shoulder just as Wagenbach turned around.

"Oh!" said Wagenbach, picking up the note. André made no effort to keep it from him.

"Top secret dispatches!" Wagenbach said, holding it up. The class laughed. They were laughing because they knew what was coming next, and I knew too. I wished I had Horst Fricke's rifle in that instant.

Wagenbach got out his reading glasses and read aloud: "Mike — Tatiana. Tatiana — Mike." He looked up first at Tatiana and then at me.

"I value your active participation in class. But if you had questions about the details of Bismarck's foreign policy, you should have just asked," he said. "There's no need to write your questions on tiny slips of paper in the hope that I accidentally find them."

This wasn't the first time he'd made this joke. He made it every time. But the class didn't care. They loved the whole charade.

There was no hope that he would stop there. There were teachers who just tore up notes, teachers who threw them in the trash or tucked them into their pockets, and then there was Wagenbach. Wagenbach was an asshole. He was the only teacher in the whole school who would read an entire text-message history when he confiscated a cell phone. It didn't matter if you begged or cried, Wagenbach read *the whole thing* aloud.

He unfolded the note solemnly, and I hoped for a miracle — like a meteorite falling from the sky and squishing Wagenbach. Or at least the bell ringing for the end of class. That would have done the trick. But of course the bell didn't ring, and of course no meteorite fell from the sky. Wagenbach's gaze swept over the class and he straightened his posture. I think he would have loved to have been an actor or cabaret performer. But he only managed to become an asshole. I mean, if only it had just been a normal old note about the usual crap. But this note contained

the first meaningful words I'd ever exchanged with Tatiana —
and perhaps the last — and Wagenbach had no right to read
them aloud for all the world to hear. .

"So, Miss Cosic writes" — and here Wagenbach paused
and nodded his chin at Tatiana as if we didn't know who she
was — "the budding literary talent Miss Cosic writes: *My
God!*" He said these words in a high-pitched squeak.

"My God," Wagenbach squeaked, *"what in the world happened to you?"*

"Jackass," I said, but it went unheard as everyone yucked
it up. Tatiana stared at her desk. Her gaze never shifted.
Wagenbach turned to me.

"And what did Mr. Klingenberg answer?"

He put his chin to his chest and spoke in a voice like a stupid cartoon bear. *"Ah, nothing special."*

The class was howling. Even Olaf, who had screwed the
whole thing up, was laughing now. I could hardly stand it.

"What polished repartee," said Wagenbach. "But will the
intellectually curious Miss Cosic be satisfied with this answer?
Or will she crave more?"

Squeaking again: *"Come on, tell me! I really want to know."*

Stupid cartoon bear: *"Well, it was like this."*

Behind his glasses, Wagenbach squinted his eyes. He could
hardly believe what he was about to read. Tatiana raised her
head a little because she didn't know my answer yet either. I
stared out the window and wondered what Tschick would do
in this situation. Probably put a completely blank look on his
face. He was better at that than I was.

Wagenbach was getting into his cartoon bear act so much
that he must not have even realized what he was reading.

"Tschick and I drove around with the Lada. We were plan-ning to drive to Wallachia, but then we flipped the car after somebody shot at us." Wagenbach paused and then continued in a normal voice. *"Then there was a police chase, a trip to the hospital. Then I crashed into an eighteen-wheeler full of pigs and my leg got all cut up . . . but anyway, no big deal."*

A few people were still laughing. Especially the three people who hadn't been at Tatiana's party. The ones who had seen me and Tschick in the Lada were more or less silent.

"Well, what do you know," said Wagenbach. "Mr. Klingenberg, the magician! Accidents, chases, gunfights. What, no murder? I guess you can't have it all."

He obviously didn't believe a word of what he had read. I guess it didn't sound very believable. And I wasn't too hot to enlighten him.

"The thing I like best about Mr. Klingenberg's exciting life isn't the cops and robbers material or that he included a chase involving — if I'm not mistaken — an *automobile* and Mr. Tschichatschow. No, no, my favorite part of this is the artful language. How concise and descriptive! How does he wrap up the whole escapade again?" He looked at me, then at the class, and then said, *"No big deal."*

Wagenbach brandished the note in front of Jennifer and Luisa, who were unlucky enough to be sitting in the front row.

"No big deal!" he repeated, starting to laugh. He probably hadn't had so much fun in a long time. Someone who was not enjoying herself at all was Tatiana. You could see it on her face. And not just because she had written me the note. She had probably figured out that my story was no made-up tall tale.

Up to this point, Wagenbach had just had fun at our expense. What we still had to look forward to was the humiliation portion of the program. The sermon. The idiotic shouting. Everyone knew it was coming, everyone was waiting for it. And when Wagenbach held up his hand, signaling for everyone to quiet down — for some reason there was no shouting, no sermon, no punishment. Instead, a meteorite really did fall from the sky. There was a knock at the door.

"Yes!" said Wagenbach.

Voormann, the principal, opened the door.

"Sorry to have to interrupt," he said. He scanned the room with a serious look on his face. "Are the students Klingenberg and Tschichatschow here?"

"Just Klingenberg," said Wagenbach.

Everyone had turned to the door, and Voormann was standing in the door frame. But you could see two uniformed officers behind him in the hall. Broad-shouldered cops in full gear, with handcuffs and pistols and all.

"Then Mr. Klingenberg needs to come with me," said Voormann.

I stood up as casually as I could — as casually as you can when your legs are shaking — and gave Wagenbach a last look. His stupid grin was gone. He actually looked a bit like a dim-witted cartoon bear, though if this were really a cartoon they would have to give him crosses for eyes and a squiggly line for a mouth now. I felt awesome despite the wobbly knees. And the shaking stopped as soon as I was outside facing the police officers.

Voormann apparently didn't know what to say. Both police-men had blank looks on their faces. One was chewing gum.

"Do you want to speak to him alone?" asked Voormann. The one chewing gum looked with surprise at Voormann, stopped chewing for a second, and shrugged. As if to say, "We don't care."

"Do you want a room where you won't be disturbed?" said Voormann.

"It won't take long," said policeman number two. "It's not a summons. We just stopped by."

Silence. Blinking. I scratched my head.

"I was in the middle of a call," Voormann finally said, tentatively. And as he walked off, "I hope everything gets cleared up."

Then it began. Number one asked, "Mike Klingenberg?"

"Yeah."

"45 Nauen Street?"

"Yeah."

"You know Andrej Tschichatschow?"

"Yes, he's a friend of mine."

"Where is he?"

"In Bleyen — the facility there."

"The juvenile detention center?"

"Yeah."

"I told you," said number two.

"How long has he been there?" asked number one, looking at me.

"Since the trial — actually before the trial."

"Have you had contact with him?"

"Has something happened to him?"

"The question was, have you had contact with him?"

"No."

"I thought he was your friend?"

"Yes."

"So?"

What on earth were they getting at? "It's a facility where you're not allowed to have any outside contact for several weeks. You're cut off from the world. You guys should know better than me."

Number one was chewing with his mouth open. This was a great relief after dealing with Wagenbach.

"What's happened?" I asked.

"A Lada," said number two. He let it sink in. A Lada. "A Lada disappeared from Annen Street."

"Kersting Street," I said.

"What?"

"We took it from Kersting Street."

"Annen Street," said the cop. "Day before yesterday. Old pile of junk. Hotwired. Found again last night near the end of one of the subway lines. Totaled."

"Yesterday," said number one. He chomped down on his gum twice. "Found it yesterday. Stolen the day before."

"So you're not talking about our Lada?"

"What do you mean by *our* Lada?"

"You know what I mean."

The gum smacked in his mouth. "We're talking about the one from Annen Street."

"What do I have to do with it?"

"That is the question."

And that's when it dawned on me that Tschick and I would be on the hook for every damn car hotwired in northeastern Berlin for the next hundred years.

But I couldn't have been the one who stole the car on Annen Street because I'd spent the day looking after old people and the evening at soccer practice. It also wasn't hard to convince the cops that Tschick couldn't have done it from a secure facility. Oddly enough, it seemed as if they had already sensed we had nothing to do with it. Especially number two, who kept saying they just wanted to spare themselves the trouble of a summons by popping by. They weren't even taking notes. I was almost disappointed. Because right at that moment, the bell rang and the door to our classroom opened. Thirty sets of eyes, including the cartoon bear's, peeked out, and it would have been somehow cooler if they'd been choking me with a nightstick. Mike Klingenberg, dangerous criminal. But unfortunately the two cops just wanted to say good-bye and be on their way.

"Shall I walk you to your car?" I asked.

Number two exploded immediately. "You trying to

show off in front of your schoolmates? You want us to cuff you too?"

That grown-up thing again. They see through you so quickly. I figured it was cooler not to try to deny it. But there was nothing more to do. I didn't want to be too pushy. After all, they'd already done plenty for me.

One day, a while later, I had to go to the principal's office to pick up a letter. An actual letter. I think in my whole life I'd gotten maybe three letters. One I'd written to myself as part of an elementary school project — we were supposed to learn about the post office or whatever. And the other two were from my grandmother before she had an Internet connection. The principal had the letter in his hand, and I could see that there was a funny sketch of a car with two stick figures in it and beams surrounding the car as if it were the sun. Under that was written:

Mike Klingenburg
Student at Hagecius Junior High School
Ninth grade (approximately)
Berlin

It was a wonder it ever reached me. But since my name was actually spelled Klingenberg and there was a Mike Klinger in fifth grade, the principal wanted to know if I knew the sender of the letter.

"Andrej Tschichatschow," I said, because the only person who could have sent it was Tschick — he must have figured out a way to get it out of the detention center despite the no-contact rule. I was really excited.

"Anselm," said the principal.

"Anselm," I said. I didn't know anyone by that name. The principal dropped his head in dismay, but after a minute I said, "Anselm Wail?"

He handed me the letter.

Crazy. Anselm Wail, high up on the mountain. I ripped it open immediately to see who had sent it. But I was too excited to read it, so I put it back in the envelope and pulled it out again an hour later when I got home.

Because of course it was from Isa. I was so excited to read it. As excited as I was when I thought it was from Tschick. I lay on my bed the entire afternoon with it, thinking about whether I was more in love with Tatiana or Isa. I wasn't sure. Seriously, I didn't know.

Hi, idiot. Did you make it to Wallachia? I'm betting you didn't. I visited my half-sister and can give you the money back now. I punched a truck driver and lost my wooden box. I had fun with you guys. It's a shame that we didn't hook up. My favorite part was eating blackberries. Next week I'm coming to Berlin. If you don't want to wait fifty years, let's meet Sunday the 29th at 5 P.M. in front of the big clock on Alexanderplatz. Kisses, Isa

I heard noises downstairs. There was a scream, a crash, and a rumble. I didn't pay attention for a long time because I figured my parents were just fighting again. I rolled onto my back and stared at the letter. Then it occurred to me that my father wasn't around because he was out looking at an apartment with Mona.

I heard more crashing and looked out the window. Nobody was in the backyard, but there was a chair floating upside down in the pool. Something else — something smaller — splashed into the water next to the chair and sank. Looked like a cell phone. I went downstairs.

My mother was standing in the frame of the backdoor hiccupping. In one hand she had a potted plant — holding it like she was choking it — and in the other hand she had a glass of whiskey.

"It's been like this for an hour," she said with despair. "The fucking hiccups won't go away."

She stood on her tiptoes and threw the plant into the pool.

"What are you doing?" I asked.

"What does it look like?" she said. "I'm not attached to this crap. And besides, I must have been out of my mind — look at the pattern on this fabric."

She held up a red-and-green-checkered throw pillow and tossed it over her shoulder into the pool.

"Remember one thing in life! Have I ever talked to you about fundamental questions? And I'm not talking about the shit with the car. I mean really fundamental questions."

I shrugged.

She gestured around the room. "None of this matters. One thing that does matter: Are you happy? That. And that alone." She paused. "Are you in love?"

I thought about it for a second.

"That's a yes," said my mother. "Forget about all that other crap."

She had looked pissed off the whole time. And she still looked pissed off, but now she also looked a little surprised. "So you're in love? And does the girl — does she love you?"

I shook my head — for Tatiana. And shrugged — for Isa.

My mother got very serious, poured herself a fresh glass of whiskey, and threw the empty bottle into the pool. Then she hugged me. She pulled the cables out of the DVD player and tossed that into the pool. Then went the remote control and the big potted fuchsia. A huge splash went up when the fuchsia landed and dark clouds of dirt bubbled up as red flower petals floated on the choppy surface.

"Ah, isn't it lovely," said my mother, beginning to cry. Then she asked me if I wanted a drink. I said I'd rather throw something into the pool.

"Help me." She went over to the sofa. We carried it over to the side of the pool and threw it in. It flipped over and its feet bobbed just below water level. Then my mother pushed the round table onto its side and rolled it in a big half circle across the terrace. It finally fell into the back of the pool. Next she took apart a lamp, put the shade on her head, and tossed the base into the pool like a shot-putter. Then the TV, CD racks, and coffee tables.

My mother had just popped a bottle of champagne across the terrace and put the spraying bottle up to her lips when the first policeman came around the corner of the house into the backyard. He tensed, then relaxed when my mother removed the lampshade and greeted him with a bow, holding out the lampshade like a feather cap. She could barely stand upright. I stood by the side of the pool holding the comfy chair that matched the sofa.

"The neighbors called," said the police officer.

"Those snooping Stasi assholes," my mother said, putting the lampshade back on her head.

"Do you live here?" asked the policeman.

"Sure do," said my mother. "And you, sir, are on our property." She went into the living room and came back out with an oil painting.

While the cop was saying something about the neighbors, disturbing the peace, and suspicion of vandalism, my mother held the painting above her head with both hands like a hang glider and sailed into the pool. She did it well. And she looked cool doing it. She came across like somebody whose favorite thing in the world was hang gliding into pools using paintings. I'm pretty sure the cops would happily have hang glided in after her if they hadn't been on duty. I let myself fall into the pool with the comfy chair. The water was lukewarm. I felt my mother reaching for my hand as I sank. Together with the chair, we sank to the bottom and then looked up from there at the iridescent, glittering surface of the water, with furniture and other dark shapes floating in it. I know exactly what went through my mind right then, as I held my breath and looked up. I thought that everybody at school was probably going to start calling me Psycho again. And that I didn't care if they did. I thought that there were worse things than having an alcoholic mother. I thought that it wouldn't be long now until I was allowed to visit Tschick at the detention center. And I thought of Isa's letter. And of Horst Fricke and his carpe diem.

I thought of the storm over the wheat field, of nurse Hanna, and the smell of gray linoleum. I thought that I would never have experienced any of it without Tschick, and thought about what a cool summer it had been — the best summer ever. All of that went through my mind as we held our breath and looked through the bubbles and shimmering surface at the two perplexed policemen who were now bending over the pool and talking to each other in a muted, distant language, in another world. And I was insanely happy. Because you can't hold your breath forever, but you can hold it for a pretty long time.

The Absolutely True Diary of a Part-time INDIAN

SHERMAN ALEXIE

WINNER OF THE NATIONAL BOOK AWARD

'Son,' Mr P said, 'you're going to find more and more hope the farther and farther you walk away from this sad, sad, sad reservation.'

So Junior, who is already beaten up regularly for being a skinny kid in glasses, goes to the rich white school miles away. Now he's a target there as well. How he survives all this is an absolute shining must-read, and a triumph of the human spirit.

'Excellent in every way, poignant and really funny and heartwarming and honest and wise and smart.'
NEIL GAIMAN

9781842708446   £6.99

EVERYBODY JAM
ALI LEWIS

Shortlisted for the Carnegie Medal

Danny Dawson lives in the middle of the Australian outback. His older brother Jonny was killed in an accident last year but no one ever talks about it.

And now it's time for the annual muster. The biggest event of the year on the cattle station, and a time to sort the men from the boys. But this year things will be different: because Jonny's gone and Danny's determined to prove he can fill his brother's shoes; because their fourteen-year-old sister is pregnant; because it's getting hotter and hotter and the rains won't come; because cracks are beginning to show ...

'What an incredible debut. Lewis brings rough poetry and raw poignancy to this coming-of-age tale. I loved it.'
Keith Gray, author of *Ostrich Boys*

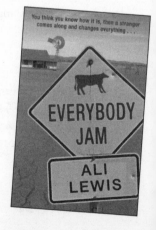

9781849392488 £6.99

OUT OF
SHADOWS

Jason Wallace

**WINNER OF THE COSTA CHILDREN'S BOOK AWARD,
THE BRANFORD BOASE AWARD AND THE UKLA BOOK AWARD**

Zimbabwe, 1980s
The war is over, independence has been won and Robert
Mugabe has come to power offering hope, land and freedom
to black Africans. It is the end of the Old Way and the start
of a promising new era.

For Robert Jacklin, it's all new: new continent, new country,
new school. And very quickly he learns that for some of his
classmates, the sound of guns is still loud, and their battles
rage on . . . white boys who want their old country back,
not this new black African government.

Boys like Ivan. Clever, cunning Ivan.
For him, there is still one last battle
to fight, and he's taking it right
to the very top.

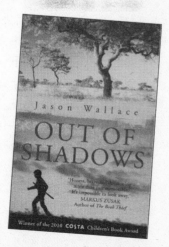

'*Honest, brave and devastating,* Out of
Shadows *is more than just memorable.
It's impossible to look away.*'
Markus Zusak, author of
The Book Thief

9781849390484 £7.99